Beyond the Shadow

Beyond the Shadow

LaJoyce Martin

Beyond the Shadow

by LaJoyce Martin

© 2002, Word Aflame Press
Hazelwood, MO 63042-2299

ISBN 1-56722-584-5

Cover Design by Paul Povolni

Covert Art by J. William Myers

All Scripture quotations in this book are from the King James Version of the Bible unless otherwise identified.

Printed in United States of America

Printed by

WORD AFLAME®PRESS
8855 DUNN ROAD
HAZELWOOD, MO 63042-2299

Contents

	The Story	7
CHAPTER 1	The Shadow.	9
CHAPTER 2	The Compromise	17
CHAPTER 3	The Forgotten Purse.	25
CHAPTER 4	Missed Connection.	33
CHAPTER 5	On to the City	39
CHAPTER 6	The Dress	47
CHAPTER 7	The Inn	53
CHAPTER 8	The Clock Salesman.	61
CHAPTER 9	Nelson's Visit.	69
CHAPTER 10	The Convert.	75
CHAPTER 11	The Promise	81
CHAPTER 12	The Discovery	87
CHAPTER 13	Surprise Guest.	93
CHAPTER 14	Missing Papers.	97
CHAPTER 15	Change	103
CHAPTER 16	Roommate	109
CHAPTER 17	Annie.	113
CHAPTER 18	The Funeral	119
CHAPTER 19	The Birthday	125
CHAPTER 20	The Fleeing of the Shadow	131
CHAPTER 21	A Joyous Day.	137
CHAPTER 22	Travel Plans	143
CHAPTER 23	Beyond the Shadow	147

The Story

It won't be long now, Trudy Briggs . . .

Trudy talked to herself in a frantic effort to squelch the mutiny of a soul that lusted for luxury. Too long she had been crushed by the iron fist of the commonplace and by the cold hand of poverty. An observer versed in human nature might have recognized the gleam in her eyes as greed for money—the root of all evil.

The woman hated being poor. She had grown tired of patching clothes, pinching pennies, and pulling bolls. For almost eighteen years, she had schemed, plotted, and planned to be rich. Now she had but four months to wait. She would have china dishes, a ball gown, and a fringed surrey. She'd entertain with elaborate banquets and teas and social soirees.

The documents—her "ticket" to wealth—were in her purse. They went with her everywhere. She dared not leave them behind.

In case the house burned . . .

In the event they were stolen . . .

Lest the children find them . . .

It had not been an easy seventeen years and eight months. She had tolerated a child that she had resented since the day of her birth—indeed, even before her birth. This girl was a problem, and a dangerous one as well.

Trudy hadn't wanted the girl. She had been in love with Tom; she had wanted Tom. But she hadn't wanted his child. Not under the circumstances.

Yet she wanted the money.

Sylene's father, Tom, had been killed in an oil field accident. A well-insured man, he left the child that he had never seen a vast sum of money—some thirty thousand dollars—to be dispensed when she turned eighteen. Knowing that his job was high risk, Tom had seen to the baby's future.

According to the legal affidavit, the child's mother would share in the benefits. And Trudy had the birth certificate, signed by the doctor, to prove that she was Sylene's mother. The chickens were in the coop, and the gate was closed.

Sylene, a shy and unassuming daughter, hadn't a hint that she stood at the vortex of the storm in the Briggs household. She didn't know why Trudy Briggs showed blatant partiality to her brothers and sisters, nor did she understand the poorly veiled hostility of her mother. She only knew that a Shadow stalked her, sabotaging her happiness and destroying her peace of mind.

Would she ever be free of the Shadow?

CHAPTER One

The Shadow

Forty dollars! What a fortune!

The bounteous gift supplied Sylene with a reason for existence, a vested hope. "I can buy land," she decided, "or order books. Or, perhaps, I can purchase a wardrobe presentable for employment."

For a speck of time, the feel of the money in her hand throttled the other feeling, a formless and shifting phantom she had christened "the Shadow." For as long as she could remember, the Shadow came and went—and often roosted—of its own accord. It was like a second "self" who kept the first self in a prison, robbing her joy. Now, with her new prospect, the Shadow cowered in the background.

In a way, she had earned the benefaction, she reckoned. But she certainly hadn't expected it. Called by the executrix of the deceased invalid she had tended for two years, Sylene discovered that the old lady had bequeathed the funds in her will "to Sylene Briggs, a sweet and worthy girl." Forty dollars! No one dreamed that the poor, aged neighbor was so wealthy.

Then the Shadow lashed back, more haunting than ever, when the windfall was unfairly taken from Sylene. The door that had opened upon a new world had abruptly closed again. There would be no land. No books. No clothes. Not only was her hope depleted, but her mind, her spirit, and her will were also drained, for the bravest of mortals can be reduced to a mere shell of humanity by long protracted mistreatment skillfully applied.

"You shall give me every penny of that money!" demanded Trudy Briggs when she learned of the legacy. "Have I reared a daughter so selfish as to wish to keep for herself what the rest of the family needs?" She held out her hand, her eyes set in cold hardness.

Sylene hesitated—and paid dearly for the hesitation, her face and her heart smarting with an undeserved lash.

"He that is greedy of gain troubleth his own house. That's what the Good Book says. And the Lord knows, you've troubled this house enough," her mother hissed, engraving the words on Sylene's mind, carving them into her heart.

Had not her father arrived to intervene, the scene would likely have grown even more volatile. For when Trudy Briggs lost her temper, she found no chocks for her emotional wheels.

"Trudy, what is the problem here?" Evart Briggs asked, his voice even, authoritative.

"This money—" Trudy snarled, waving the bills in midair. "Sylene—"

Evart's jaws bunched. "Where did you get that money, Trudy?"

"It belonged to the elderly Mrs. Oakum who died. She left it to . . . *us* . . . in her will. And Sylene is trying to claim it."

Sylene had not raised her head. No words lay in the vocabulary of a seventeen-year-old to express the feeling that assaulted her, wrenching and inexplicable. There arose, like water rising in the horse trough with the heavy spring rains, the sense of rejection, of unwarranted guilt.

The Shadow was coming near, and she could not stop it. The thing had stalked her ever since she had become conscious of herself as a being. This strange depth of need, something beyond herself, a void that was a live thing, squirmed in her soul. She felt as though a part of her was not there, was missing. And she could do nothing about it. The emptiness must be filled or . . .

Nothing within the grasp of her mind could express the alternative that lay beyond the thought.

Now she stood still, hearing her father's questions, her mother's misdirected answers, wanting, even straining to turn and run. But she could not move.

"What have you to say for yourself, Sylene?" Evart asked.

Sylene swallowed quickly, trying to clear the tumbling uncertainty within her, aware yet of her stinging face. Then, to her supreme disgust, her voice broke. "It . . . it is mine. The money belongs to me," she finished lamely, confusedly.

Her quiet tears seemed, in some obscure way, to feed Trudy's anger. "Stingy! Stingy! Stingy!" The woman moved toward the girl, but Evart stepped between them. "Can you believe, Evart, that we reared a child who would put her own selfish wishes ahead of the younger children?

Why, she planned to keep *all forty dollars!*"

"I . . . planned to use it . . . wisely . . ." Even to her own ears, Sylene's defense sounded feeble.

Trudy ignored her. "And just for that, she shall have none of the money."

"We will be fair, Trudy." Evart's tone observed the courtesies of their relationship, but there was no yielding. "Since through her acquaintance with Mrs. Oakum we were granted this great benevolence, Sylene shall be given her part."

"No, she shan't! I shall have my way this time, Evart Briggs. You have taken Sylene's side against me all her life. The older she gets, the more you cotton to her. Don't think I haven't noticed!" Bitterness grew stronger on her malice-tipped tongue. "But this is one time—"

Would her father win? Sylene's heart beat with sick helplessness.

"You may go to your room, Sylene," Evart said, "while your mother and I get to the heart of the matter." He patted her shoulder, and when she looked up, he smiled kindly. "We'll straighten the problem out. Satisfactorily, I'm sure."

Sylene left, but she didn't go to her room. She wanted no prying questions, no snide remarks from her sisters— sixteen-year-old Ann Marie and fourteen-year-old Rosalind—who shared the cramped sleeping quarters with her. Instead, she made her way to the frayed hammock, suspended between two mulberry trees in the back yard. She needed a solitary place to think, to sift through the ashes of her mother's vagary for a grain of reason.

And think she did—back and back—though her thoughts brought no resolution. At age fifteen, Sylene had finished the eighth grade, the highest level of education offered by the nearby country school. In the ensuing months, she had spent most of her time with the ailing Mrs. Oakum, who claimed her "days were numbered." The old woman's home was Sylene's sanctum, a covert from her mother's unreasonable demands. She didn't mind emptying Mrs. Oakum's chamber pot, but she resented Trudy's demand that she do the same chore for Ann Marie. Why?

The Shadow came less often while she was at Mrs. Oakum's residence, and it was more easily tamed there. Mrs. Oakum loved Sylene, showering her with kindness. In spite of the elderly woman's weak and infirm condition, they talked and played games together with genial rapport.

Then the childless widow used up her quota of days and departed for a painless interim, leaving Sylene with the disputed forty dollars. No doubt, she intended to bring Sylene utmost happiness. Instead, she had occasioned a bruised face and a crushed heart.

Had the money been left to Ann Marie, her sister would have been given every cent to squander at will. Had Rosalind been the recipient, she would have been required to share with Ann Marie. Ann Marie, a girl who knew how to flatter her mother, was Trudy's pet. What Ann Marie wanted, Ann Marie got. She had always been pampered and indulged; her path had always been made smooth under her feet. It seemed that Trudy was trying to relive her youth through Ann Marie.

Sylene's mind chafed and roiled. *Why must I, the eldest, be expected to forfeit my plans, my dreams, and my future for my woefully spoiled siblings?*

Ah, but life had ever been thus! This was the prison in which Sylene Briggs had to serve her life sentence. Tonight she would go to bed bankrupt of spirit, to awake at sunrise and retread the cheerless round of drudgery. Every other tomorrow, while life fettered her here, held a repetition of just this and nothing more.

Committing her weary body to the hassock's sway— she had bent over the flatiron for most of the day—Sylene tried to let her brain unravel in the breeze-threaded dusk. She listened to the wind's endless, mindless soughing, observed the compliant bending of the tree branches, and coaxed her better judgment once again to bow to her fate. For her own preservation, her spirit must cease groping for an explanation to her mother's injustice. She must accept her lot in life, burying her own misgivings. She would let her soul grow quiet in the rhythmic adjustment of the moment.

As Sylene rocked slowly back and forth, the old remembered sense of need washed over her again, faintly at first, then with a deepening of possession until she shook with its force. It lay at the pit of her soul. Nothing—not the anger at her mother, or the detachment that bathed her now, not the complaining of her bruised cheek, or her disappointment—nothing could stand before the hollowness. Within her was only this vast emptiness.

The fingers of sunset touched the old house's screened porch, and suddenly Sylene felt everything previously familiar to her become strange in that moment. Her eyes panned the beleaguered dwelling turned sickly gray by years of sun and rain. The house seemed to huddle in the gathering shadows with melancholic despair. Its walls looked over the unproductive acres around it. Seasons of relentless planting had taken their toll on the land that lay beyond, and now, less than three years before the turn of the new century, revenue from the crops scarcely put food on the table. This was the property her parents had leased her entire life, but at once she knew it wasn't a factor in her past or present.

Yes, this was the house she occupied, but she was someone else—a girl, or the ghost of a girl, who lived there, slept there, had head colds and washed her stockings there. To Ann Marie, it was home. To Rosalind, it was home. To the boys, nine-year-old Windsor and five-year-old Chuckie, it was home.

To Sylene, it was the Shadow's home . . .

CHAPTER TWO

The Compromise

Night hours were the worst. Sylene lay on her lumpy mattress, staring into the darkness as the last wisps of a forgotten dream dissolved. Her mind, groping through sleep, saw the room as a well of dark water in which she had drowned, along with the drowned mirror, the drowned washstand, and the drowned granite wash pan.

A remnant of wind, a thin susurration of complaint, chased about the corners of the house. A star peered down at her through the open window, and she wondered if this might be God watching her. Did God think her stingy or greedy for wanting what was rightfully hers? Did He care that her hopes were dashed?

Outside, a dark mass of lilac bushes took shape in the reddening east, becoming a dusky reality. A cock crowed. The smell of night and the coming dawn commingled. Another day was being born, another dreaded day. Life would be as it had always been. Wearisome. Perplexing. Onerous. Sylene shivered.

Breakfast was her assignment. She scrambled from bed, smoothing the covers with one quick gesture, and reached for her only dress, a faded feed sack gown that hardly touched her blossoming body anywhere. As light seeped into the room, her feet felt their way to the kitchen, leaving behind the shabby rug, the patched blue bedspread, and the cracked dressing table. Ann Marie and Rosalind slept on.

"Good morning, Sylene." Evart sat in the semidarkness, drinking his coffee. He looked as if he'd slept little.

Sylene turned her face away.

"I hope that you rested well?"

"Well enough, sir." Her tone made no effort to bridge the infinite distance that separated them.

Yesterday's strain seemed enhanced by the morning light, and even as Sylene's hand reached for the pewter skillet to make gravy, she sensed that her mother had come in, and she stiffened.

Trudy walked past her, her hands straightening her best skirt. "Be quick about breakfast, Sylene. We have a big day ahead of us."

Sylene stoked the fire but said nothing.

"Is the wagon ready, Evart?" Trudy spoke to her husband, but her eyes were upon Sylene. There was, as she spoke, a preoccupation in her manner as if her mind was busy with other matters. "And did you tell Sylene of your plans?"

"We plan to go to Fort Worth today, Sylene."

Good, Sylene rejoiced inwardly. *I shall have the day to myself.*

"I hope that you have a pleasant trip," she said aloud, supposing that some response was required of her.

18

"You are going, too."

Sylene's stomach turned. "All of us are going? I will be happy to stay here and let the others go in my place."

Trudy's eyes bored into her sharply. "Only you and your father and I are going, Sylene. Ann Marie will tend the boys. She's old enough. Some girls are married by age sixteen. Evart insists that you have a new dress."

"Will Ann Marie and Rosalind be pleased?"

"No, and I am not pleased, but until Evart's stubborn persistence is out of the way, we cannot see to the needs of anyone else. He insists that you shall have priority. He will have it no other way."

"I will be glad to stay home. Truly, I will. Take the other children."

Evart banged his coffee cup on the table with a noisy thud. "Sylene, you will have a new dress first. You will be birthdaying before long, and you need a pretty, store-bought frock. Your mother and I reached a little compromise. I told her that since you were the chief cause of our getting this nice booty, it would only be right that you be rewarded." His manner softened. "You would like a fetching outfit, now, wouldn't you?"

"Oh yes, sir!"

Evart touched his napkin to his lips. "The journey will take most of the day."

"Is it a very long way to Fort Worth, Father?"

"It's several miles. We will take the wagon into Bruceville and catch the stagecoach on from there." He paused. "Don't you think it is time that you see a bit of this world?"

Excitement blazed in Sylene's veins. What would it be like to go to a real city? To have a fitted dress? *The dress*

19

will be just the right size. It will be blue with a wide sash and puffed sleeves . . .

But her thoughts were already dying, bled by deeper conflicts. She would not be allowed to make a selection that would pique Ann Marie's envy. Ann Marie would have the gorgeous dress. Sylene's garment would likely be brown or gray, shapeless, and made of cheap muslin. That's why, Sylene concluded, that Trudy insisted on going along—to monitor the purchase.

One by one, the rest of the family filtered in for the morning meal. Sylene handed Chuckie his cup of warmed milk and broke a biscuit and ladled syrup over its middle for Windsor, smearing it with a methodical wave of her spoon. She'd memorized each child's preference.

Ann Marie ambled in, armored with her chronic insolence. "What's the occasion?" she asked, staring at her mother's attire.

"We're going to Fort Worth," Evart told her.

"Goody."

"You're not going."

"I *am so* going."

"You're not going."

"Mama!—"

"Darling, we will take you next week and buy you the most fetching dress in Texas! You and Rosalind be sweeties now and stay with the boys. Mama will see that you are well rewarded."

Trudy hardly touched her food. "I'll get my purse and hat," she announced. "We don't want to miss the coach." She bustled from the room.

"I'll have a vanity set when I go shopping," Ann Marie demanded. "A black and silver one with lots of lip and eye

paints to go with my pretty, new frocks."

"I want new slippers," added Rosalind. "Dancing slippers."

"A spinner top for me," put in Windsor, shoving a great, dripping bite of biscuit into his mouth. "Who wants clothes?"

"And a monkey for me. A real live one," chimed Chuckie. "One time, Sylene read me a story about a monkey named Banana. He could eat hundreds of peanuts without stopping." Chuckie's memory was so inaccurate and his imagination so acute that the original tale was lost under the mountain of his own invention.

Everyone laughed except Sylene. She wasn't listening.

"Did we get rich all at once?" questioned Ann Marie.

"We did come by a little money," Evart said, "thanks to Sylene. That's why we are going to buy her an outfit first, children. She will soon be grown up, and we want her to look nice."

Ann Marie scowled. "I'm not a 'children,' and I act more grown-up than Sylene does. I'm the one who needs to look pretty, for I have five boyfriends and Sylene doesn't have any!" Her voice was deprecating. "And I don't think it's fair that she gets to choose first!"

With a lecture set on his lips, Evart started to reply when Trudy came back hugging her black purse. "You are to clean the table and wash the dishes, Ann Marie."

"Mama! It's not fair!—"

"And boys, mind that you behave. If you don't, you'll get a switching when we return. Is that clear? Let's be on our way, Evart. We've no time to dally. Come along, Sylene."

The drive to the station was quiet. Sitting in close

21

proximity to her mother, Sylene discovered, bedded in her heart like muddy water settled in a glass, a loathing, unacknowledged before, for the woman. The realization of it was as sudden as the slap had been the evening before. Surprise curdled her thoughts, and the bruise on her face set up a dim pain that was not at all physical. Long minutes passed before the biting resentment abated, and when it did, Sylene felt herself no longer a girl. She had become, in some way, a woman.

As they approached the station in Bruceville, bright sunlight beat against the dim windows of the small depot, mirroring the waiting room and its occupants. Already, the room was crowded. Evart turned the horse and wagon to the liveryman, and the three of them went inside.

Assorted sizes of people filled the long, stiff benches or leaned, with travel cases piled around them, against the walls. A smell of human bodies—the pungent scent that even clean folks emit in close quarters—hung in the poorly ventilated room.

Trudy hurried to the ticket seller's cage to purchase their passes and returned presently. "This is for the round trip." She placed a cardboard square in Sylene's hand, keeping the other two in her own. "Don't lose it," she warned, as if Sylene were Chuckie's age.

An icy tremor slid down Sylene's spine. Excitement, dread, and fear merged. Her fingernails cut into her palms, and prickles inched along her scalp. She had never been to the city, to a boutique, or to a millinery shop. She had never had a dress of refined fabric. That her mother would allow her a truly becoming dress was beyond her comprehension. *If she does, Ann Marie will fly into a tizzy so that the joy of wearing it will be robbed,* con-

sidered Sylene. *Why must life be so complicated?*
Eventually, the coach skidded in, sliding to a halt with clatter and flourish, and travelers began lining up at the door. Trudy tugged at Evart's arm. "The coach is here, Evart." Sylene followed closely behind them.

With a sweep of his hand, the porter drew an invisible line between Sylene and her parents. "Sorry, but we will have to divide the passengers here," he said. "One of you must wait for the next coach, which will be arriving in a quarter hour. The two coaches will get to the Fort Worth station at approximately the same time. One travels the eastern route through Waco and Hillsboro; the other goes west through Cleburne." Panic rose in Sylene's throat. She tried to cross the invisible line.

Evart stepped back. "I will travel with Sylene, Trudy."

Trudy's words cracked like a whip. "Evart, Sylene is nearing eighteen. She isn't a baby anymore. You will ride with your wife, and Sylene will come on the next coach."

The driver signaled them to move along. "If you are coming with us, ma'am, you must board immediately. We are on a strict schedule."

"We will be waiting for you at the Fort Worth station, Sylene," Trudy nodded, pushing Evart ahead of her.

Sylene chopped down the answering flare of anxiety that welled like dry cotton in her throat. She touched her mother's sleeve. "Would . . . could you ride with me?"

"You are a big girl now, Sylene. I should think you would enjoy acting your age. Why, Rosalind would be happy to make a solo trip, and she's but fourteen! Perhaps we should buy you a bib rather than a dress!" Sylene felt the scald of her mother's contempt, and she was ashamed that she had let the hem of her fear show from beneath her resolve.

Then the first load of passengers was gone, leaving the station quieter. Those who had come to meet travelers scattered to the yard and beyond while others awaited the arrival of family and friends on the incoming coach. Who was coming and who was going was but a calculated guess, yet it was apparent that the demon of terror had attacked no one but Sylene.

With its dire suspense, the quarter hour wait took on eternal proportions. What if the second coach did not arrive on time? What if it, too, was overcrowded? What if. . . ?

But the stage pulled into the station at the appointed time. In her eagerness to board, Sylene almost missed the step.

CHAPTER Three

The Forgotten Purse

Discomfited, Sylene took a seat by a window, paying no heed to her fellow travelers. Why couldn't her mother have stayed behind to ride with her? If Ann Marie had asked . . .

The door closed, and Sylene nervously awaited the forward motion of the coach. But at its first lurch, a man dashed from the depot, swinging his arms, causing the driver to bring the vehicle to an abrupt stop. "Does this belong to the young lady?" Trudy's black handbag dangled from his right hand.

"It is my mother's purse," Sylene nodded.

The man dropped the bag into her lap.

"Thank you. I shall take it for her."

She wondered if her mother had missed it, and in some vague way, its presence calmed her.

They were soon off. Sylene supposed hers was the western coach as she studied the framed map, tacked on a side panel, detailing the route. Various thin lines represented rivers and railroads, and small squares portrayed villages that they would pass through before reaching their destination.

There wasn't much to see along the way—unbroken meadows that stretched for miles ahead—and before long the short night took its toll on the weary traveler. She fell asleep to the music of the road's monotonous chant.

Long and hard she slept. Awakened by a travel announcement that struck brutally through her consciousness, she heard only the conclusion of the news, ". . . to Fort Worth." The coach was slowing, and she supposed that her journey was finished, that her nap had made the trip seem brief. Her parents would be waiting, and the three of them would begin the business of shopping. Trudy would be relieved to see her purse which, no doubt, held the money.

The car ground to a stop, and Sylene disembarked, along with a young man seated behind her. The other passengers stayed aboard. After a fleet halt, the coach headed north, and Sylene followed the gravel pathway, beaten and tired from the imprint of many feet, to the depot to join her parents.

But they were not there . . .

She sought for the ticket agent to make inquiry about them, finding no one behind the counter. In fact, the building was vacant except for a sweet faced woman who obviously had come to meet the young gentleman.

"I'm glad God gave you a safe trip home, Nelson." The woman kissed his cheek. "I prayed for you."

"Thank you, Mother," he returned.

Wild terror tore at Sylene's mind. As vividly as if someone had laid a frozen hand on her shoulder, she felt the cold clutch of hysteria. Where could her mother and father be? The man and his mother were on the verge of departing, and she would be left alone in a strange and deserted building. She couldn't let that happen!

"Pardon me," she said as she moved toward them.

The soft-eyed woman turned and smiled. "Would you like for us to wait with you until your ride comes?"

"They were to meet me here."

"Who is coming for you, dear? I know most of the people in our little town."

"I . . . that is, my parents said they would be here. I suppose the other coach has arrived? Or—"

"What other coach, dear? There is but one coach a day that stops here."

At a great cost, Sylene held back tears of fright. "But the man said—you see, my parents came on one coach and I on the other. We were to meet in Fort Worth—"

"But this isn't the Fort Worth station. This is the Cleburne depot. Fort Worth is thirty-six miles farther."

"I am not at the . . . the right place?"

"If your destination is Fort Worth, you have a ways to go."

"Oh, then I surely must go on! Mother and Father won't know what happened to me!"

"There will not be another coach to take you until this time tomorrow. I'm afraid you'll have to lay over. But I'm sure your parents will guess what happened and await you there."

"Oh, I have caused so much trouble for them! Mother will be very angry with me." Tears came now, big splashing drops, unbidden, eliciting a look of pity from the observing woman.

"Anyone can make a mistake, especially if you are not accustomed to the route. I dare say your mother will be so glad to see you that she couldn't possibly scold. That's the way mothers are."

"But . . . what will I do?" A fresh volley of tears fell.

"Don't fret, dear girl. God has His design in everything. You can come home with Nelson and me, and Nelson will see you back to the station tomorrow." She clucked. "You and I aren't so far apart in size that you can't wear one of my own nightgowns."

"Oh no." Sylene drew in her breath with a sharp gasp. "I couldn't leave the station. I will just . . . just wait here."

"I would not rest with a lone girl spending the night in a public building," the lady said. "It isn't safe, I'm afraid. Your parents wouldn't approve."

"But I could not impose upon your goodness. You don't know me, and I don't know you."

The woman patted her arm. "Our name is Curtis. We are Christians, and you can trust us. In fact, God has chosen my Nelson to preach His Word. He has been saved since he was ten years old."

Saved. The word gouged at Sylene's mind. She had heard it before, but she didn't know what it meant. Once she had tried to talk to her father about God, but his words had been hesitant, embarrassed, as if the matter were in some way an indecent subject.

"I've made a pot of soup," Mrs. Curtis was saying. "Nelson's favorite. You must be quite hungry after your long trip."

Yes, she was hungry.

They walked across the small town together, the

Curtises pulling her into conversation. "And what should we call you?" Nelson asked.

"My name is Sylene Briggs."

"Sylene. That is a beautiful name. I believe you boarded at the Bruceville station?"

"Yes, my family lives on a farm near there."

Sylene did not do her part to sustain the dialogue. She was still troubled, her emotions in a chaotic state. Trudy would be furious that she had exited at the wrong station and would flog her with harsh words. Why had she been so stupid as to leave the coach prematurely? She had occasioned a hardship for everybody.

Preoccupied, she missed the sight of picket fences, flower gardens, and back yards where little children played and washing hung on the lines. She could not have told how far it was to the Curtis's small frame house or how to get back to the station. But once inside the Curtis residence, her spirit was soothed with the peaceful atmosphere.

Mrs. Curtis fussed over her. "It isn't every day that Nelson and I have such a lovely guest. Why, I think God must have sent you our way. We love visitors and have few. There's just the two of us, you see. Nelson's father went on to be with the Lord two years ago. We were only granted ten short years together, Ned and I, but they were wonderful years."

Mrs. Curtis talked on, "Nelson's parents died when he was an infant, and his uncle took him. Ned was caring for his nephew single-handedly when I came along. I fell in love with both of them! Ned and I had no children of our own. I felt truly deprived of a daughter, but I guess I'll have to be satisfied with a daughter-in-law, though Nelson has been in no hurry to oblige me. He is twenty-three, quite an old man I remind him."

She brought Sylene buttered bread and a mug of warm soup. "Here, just you rest, dear, and please don't worry. God is in control of everything. Have you a hobby?"

"I like to read."

"Oh, that's Nelson's hobby, too! I tell him he will be blind if he doesn't slow down. Books, books, books. I tease him that people would be more interesting, but he just grins and says when he gets tired of a book he can close it!"

"The soup is delicious, Mrs. Curtis."

"Most anything tastes good when one is hungry. You had to get up quite early to make your trip, did you not?"

"I awoke at four thirty."

"Then you will want to retire early, I'm sure. We'll have our devotions when you have finished the soup. Nelson and I always finish the day with prayer and Bible reading. It is a habit of ours."

Sylene held her tongue, afraid that she might say the wrong thing. Whatever this ritual might be, they were comfortable with it. There was no strangeness, no question in it for them. She alone stood outside the blessing. She and the Shadow.

At the end of the meal, Nelson picked up the great family Bible and opened it. Clearing his throat, he read aloud: "Come unto me, all ye that labour and are heavy laden, and I will give you rest." He kept reading, as if he were reading solely for her benefit: "Take my yoke upon you, and learn of me; for I am meek and lowly in heart: and ye shall find rest unto your souls. For my yoke is easy, and my burden is light."

Who was speaking these beautiful words?

After a while, Nelson closed the Book with gentle hands. "That is God's invitation to us," he said. "Now, shall we pray?"

Sylene sat, stilled and listening to Nelson's prayer. "And, heavenly Father, we ask that You give rest to our lovely guest. Let her body and soul be refreshed by Thy love and Thy Spirit in our humble home. . . ."

Sylene heard his voice, but she watched him, too. A whirlpool of thoughts tossed to and fro in her mind, and they were not all spiritual thoughts. Dark hair. Broad shoulders. Husky voice. Here was a true gentleman. What would it be like to spend the rest of her life with him?

Without warning, something stirred within Sylene. It seized her heart and held her captive. Nothing she had ever imagined, nothing she had ever felt had prepared her for this moment. *Oh, I love him!* she thought. *Right now, I have fallen in love with Nelson Curtis. No one else matters; nothing else matters. Let this perfect evening go on forever. Don't let it ever stop . . .*

No one warned her that love could bite so hard. She had never known the depth and breadth of it—nor the desolation. The hurt went deeper, seeping into the marrow of her soul. No! She could never yield to the voice of her heart. Romance was not for her—because of the Shadow.

CHAPTER Four

Missed Connection

"My purse!" Disembarking at the Fort Worth station, Trudy froze on the steps of the coach. "Evart, I forgot my purse. Please get it for me."

Evart glanced back. "I don't see your purse in the coach, Trudy."

"Look under the seat."

Evart stepped aside while the other passengers filed out, then searched the vehicle's interior. "Your purse is not here."

The driver had climbed from his box. "My purse—" Trudy began, but he interrupted.

"You did not have a purse when you boarded, ma'am."

"I . . . I didn't?" She pounded her head with the heel of her hand. "Then I must have left it at the depot."

"If you left it there, ma'am, there is no call to worry. The agent will keep it for you. They have a safe box for any luggage that is inadvertently left behind."

"We must go back at once, Evart."

"We shall wait until Sylene arrives."

"We could leave word for Sylene."

"No, we will wait."

"The western line should be coming in any minute, sir," said the driver. "We have a little game going to see how closely we can correlate our arrivals. James, the other driver, has even been known to beat me here. He doesn't waste time at his stops. The next coach south leaves early in the morning. Have a good day."

Trudy's voice rose. "The money was in that purse, Evart. If we have to be here awhile, we don't even have the coins for a loaf of bread! What will we do—?"

"A fast from food will not ruin us, Trudy."

"But without money, we will have to sit in the station all night, you and Sylene and I."

"That will not send us to our graves either."

"This is serious, Evart."

"What do you expect me to do about it, Trudy? It was not I who left the purse. A woman should keep up with her own baggage."

"I should have known!" groused Trudy. "Anytime Sylene is involved, there is trouble. It has been this way since the day she was born!"

Early in their marriage, Evart tried to mitigate Trudy's moods, but he had learned that they were like fevers that had to run their course. With little or no reason behind them, they spread formlessly, seeking a reason, needing an irritant around which the infection of bad temper could collect. If he spoke, even in sympathy, her peeve took shape instantly around his protest. He was to blame, or Sylene was to blame, or the weather was to blame. If he bridled his tongue, though, her anger would come to a head and burst. Now, the muscles ridged in his neck as he clamped his lips tightly, waiting for the eruption.

However, before her ire could come to a core, the west line coach rumbled to a standstill before the door. "There she is," Evart cheered, moving toward the entrance. "See, we didn't have long to wait after all."

The passengers straggled off the car: A mother carrying a child whose cherubic face rested against her shoulder in sleep, a man leaning on an ornate cane, an impatient businessman.

"She will be next," Evart said after the exodus of each patron. But Sylene was not among them. Finally came the coachman, dusting his trousers and sleeves as if he had been at the bottom of the heap.

"Sir," Evart approached the driver, "is this the stage from Bruceville?"

He nodded, closing the coach. "Yes, sir."

"We were expecting our daughter."

"A lass about twenty?"

"Yes."

"She got off at one of the interim stops." He paused. "I've forgotten where."

"She left the coach alone?"

"Well, no. There was a handsome young man who got off at the same station."

"And there won't be another coach coming in?"

"Not today."

"Do you suppose she went back home?" Trudy asked Evart. "I don't think she really wanted to come—"

"Yes, she wanted to come, Trudy. She wanted a new dress. She just got off at the wrong place. You should have let me ride along with her."

"She has a return ticket. She's no infant; if she's lost, she'll find her way home."

"You don't suppose—?"

"No, the young man the driver mentioned did not coax her off the coach, Evart. I know what you're thinking, but a handsome young man would have no interest in Sylene. She's homely and backward. Now, if it had been Ann Marie—"

"Sylene is a beautiful young lady!"

"Only in your eyes."

Evart dodged the barb. "Let's go inside and sit, Trudy. We have a long wait for the next coach."

As the evening unwound its pattern of hours and they were left alone in the building, Trudy's complaint about her hunger turned to nagging. Evart went outside and found an apple tree laden with green fruit. *If bellyache she must*, he chuckled to himself, *I'll give her something to bellyache about.* Trudy wolfed down three knotty, green apples.

"I remember now, Evart. I remember setting my purse on a bench to distribute the tickets," she said. "It will be there. I'll be glad to get it back, for Ann Marie would be dreadfully disappointed if I lost the money and she didn't get her vanity set. All she thinks about is prettying herself up; she's at that age."

"Why did Sylene insist that the money from Mrs. Oakum was hers, Trudy? I still don't understand. It isn't like Sylene—"

"It was because of a silly little note that Mrs. Oakum left when she died. She said the forty dollars was for 'Sylene Briggs, a sweet and worthy girl.' I saw the note myself. And they called it a will! Well, you know as well as

I that our impartial neighbor didn't mean that Sylene should have the whole forty dollars! The old lady knew that we had other children—"

"Was the note signed?"

"Yes."

"Then it was legal, Trudy. If Mrs. Oakum specified that Sylene have the money—all of it—it belongs to Sylene by law. I'm afraid you didn't tell me the whole story."

"Evart Briggs, there is no way a mother could stand by and see one child take all the money for herself and the others have none!"

"Sylene didn't *take* the money, Trudy. It was *given* to her. You took her money, and if she wishes, she can have you arraigned in court for theft."

"A daughter that I have raised? Take me to court? A daughter call me a thief?"

"She could if she wished."

"She wouldn't."

"Of course, she wouldn't. But now that I know the circumstances, I will defend her rights. If Mrs. Oakum gave the money to her, she shall have it. The entire forty dollars—or what is left of it. It belongs to her."

"She shan't have it!" With her temper escalating, Trudy shrieked the words in a high pitched voice.

Evart didn't raise his. "She shall."

"Can you imagine, Evart, what she might spend the money for?" A familiar nervous twitch began to pull at the corners of Trudy's mouth. "Why, she might buy books."

"She can spend the money as she wishes," Evart said. "It is hers."

"Ann Marie and Rosalind would cry if she didn't buy some pretty clothes for them." She narrowed her eyes.

"And your taking Sylene's side proves something I have suspected all along. You have more than just a fatherly affection for her. You've always favored her!"

"Perhaps that is because you've always been unfair to her," he countered. "Someone has to defend her. Yes, she was sickly and cried a lot when she was small, and in contrast, Ann Marie was a pleasant baby. But that is no reason to—"

"I won't hear it! You are misjudging me. And you are interfering with my method of parenting. In asking Sylene to share her money, I am creating in her a generous spirit. The act will cause the younger children, who sometimes resent her, to admire her the more. Parenting is a tricky business, Evart, and you must allow me to do what I know is best for my children."

No matter what Evart Briggs said, he never won an argument.

CHAPTER Five

On to the City

In its porcelain holder, the candle guttered down to a dwarfed stub. Sylene sat staring at Mrs. Curtis's stiffly starched scrim curtains, acutely aware of life, love, and the bittersweet taste of solitude. She crawled beneath her quilt and lay curled for a long time thinking, *What is to become of me? When I return, I will never be happy again. I am not a child anymore. What shall I do? What is life all about?*

When her lids became leaden, she blew out the light. If only she could stay here forever, away from her mother's asperity, away from Ann Marie's jealousy, away from Rosalind's foolish prattle, away from the governing hand of the Shadow.

The sounds of reality—chirping crickets and rustling leaves and the ticking of the grandfather clock—muted and blended, sliding away with the tide of sleep that swirled around and under her. The last sound she heard was Nelson's voice: "Good night, Mother." Then the wave of blackness closed over her.

But the strangeness of her surroundings made her restless, and with each waking, her memory trolled up Nelson: his thoughtful brown eyes, his deep and gentle voice, his smile. The recall drove her loneliness so deep that she had to think quickly of something else. What would she do when night ran out? She would have several hours to spend in this house before the coach came. How would she endure Nelson's closeness?

But her worries were needless. Nelson slipped away early to help a rheumatic neighbor plant his okra, leaving the morning to the womenfolk.

"Had Nelson known that we would have company, he wouldn't have promised to help with the planting today," mentioned Mrs. Curtis.

"That is fine, Mrs. Curtis. Your son certainly has no obligation to me. Had I been more attentive, I wouldn't have missed my destination and put you folks out."

"Oh, you haven't put us out, my dear. I wish I could keep you!" Mrs. Curtis responded. "Of course, that wouldn't be fair to your own family. I do hope, though, that since God put you into our lives, you will come to see us often. I've grown quite fond of you in our short acquaintance, and I think Nelson is affected too. Both of us feel that . . . that God sent you."

At the mention of Nelson's name, Sylene looked away, thinking that Mrs. Curtis might read the truth in her eyes, the truth that told of the love she felt for her son. No one must know. Ever.

"Tell me about yourself, Sylene. About your family."

All the hurts that lay within her crowded into Sylene's throat, and she warded off the desire to blurt them to someone who might understand. She wanted to tell this motherly friend about the emotional torment, about the Shadow. But she was afraid . . .

"I am the eldest of five," she said. "I have two sisters, ages sixteen and fourteen, and two brothers, nine and five."

"How lovely! And big sister is their heroine, right?"

"Actually, Ann Marie, the sixteen year old, holds that honor."

"Why is that? Is she ill? Does she have a problem that demands special attention?"

"N . . . no," Sylene stumbled. "She just seems to be my mother's . . . choice."

"Now, that is strange. I mean, for a mother to make a difference in her children."

"I . . . I'm the black sheep." After she said it, Sylene longed to recall the admission.

"You don't seem to be rebellious."

Sylene blushed. Mrs. Curtis had misunderstood. "I didn't mean that I have been disobedient . . . or . . . or wicked. But I . . . I seem to provoke my mother and my sisters, just by *being*. My father is good to me; however, I think my mother will be glad when I am no longer a 'burden.'"

"'A burden?' Why, I can't imagine such a thing! I would give anything for a daughter! Is your mother a Christian, dear?"

"No. I don't suppose so, anyhow. We never go to church. Or read the Bible. Or pray."

"That's too bad."

"For the last two years, I have worked away from home. I've spent most of my time with an elderly lady. I think she may have been a Christian. I did her laundry and cleaned her house."

"After school?"

"I finished school when I was fifteen. Our school stopped at grade eight. Mother decided that was all the book learning I needed, though I would have loved to gain more education. Ann Marie will attend the academy, if she wishes, when she finishes school. I'm not worth the trouble or expense—"

"Oh, precious girl, don't think that for a minute! You are a golden treasure in God's eyes—and in mine, too. And do you not still work for the older lady?"

"She passed on."

"And you miss her, don't you?"

"Oh, how I miss her!" Should she bare her heart to Mrs. Curtis? "She . . . she was very kind to me, you see. She left me forty dollars in her will, and I thought . . . I had thought I could get a start in life for myself with land or books or better clothes—" Sylene looked at her shapeless, faded dress.

"And that's why you are going to Fort Worth, to get a start?"

"No, ma'am. When my mother learned about the money, she . . . she needed it . . . and she took it." The impulse to tell that her mother had struck her lasted only a second, then like an ocean breaker crashing against the shore, it receded suddenly, leaving as a backwash only a sense of shame. "However, my father insisted that I at least have a new dress. That is the purpose of our trip. My mother will see that the dress does not use much of the money."

"But, my dear," objected Mrs. Curtis, "that was not

just. For her to take your money was not a Christian thing to do! The money was yours. Mind you, I'm not speaking disparagingly of your mother. I'm speaking in terms of right and wrong. And perhaps I should say nothing at all. It is wonderful of you to forgive. You have a generous spirit."

Had she forgiven? "I wish . . . I wish I could go away." There, she had said it! Inordinate alarm swept through her. At last, she had voiced the thought that she had desperately avoided, and her own words terrified her.

Mrs. Curtis's voice was low and quiet. "Precious Sylene, you can live with me. I will be glad to have a daughter such as yourself."

Live here? What a temptation! The Briggs family wouldn't even notice that she was gone. There would be no more pretending that she didn't care about the overt slights. No more long sessions with herself to stamp out bitterness. No more raising herself painfully onto a platform of detachment—and then at the table, having some stinging remark bring the choking lump to her chest, peeling her feelings bare. What would it be like to feel valuable to someone? To anyone?

But then pictures of Nelson came to focus in the lens of her mind. "Oh, I couldn't do that!"

"The doors are open here for you. The latch is on the outside, now and for always."

What would happen if she accepted Mrs. Curtis's invitation? The unconditional love of the woman, a privilege Sylene had never known, made her wish that she might stay.

Time elapsed with fits and starts, and afternoon came with its hour of departure. At half past two, she said her

43

good-byes to her new friend. Desolation settled into a hard knot in the center of her being. The Shadow was slinking back, and how dreadful was this empty, hopeless feeling . . .

Nelson was waiting for her at the door. He took her hand, and as she walked beside him, she felt strong and safe. "I wish I had a fine buggy for you, Sylene," he said.

"I enjoy walking," she said. *With you.* She didn't say it aloud, did she? "It is such a lovely day."

"Indeed. Every day is good when we walk hand in hand with God."

She yearned to ask him about God and how one found a relationship with Him, but she couldn't find the words. She knew so little about spiritual matters that Nelson might think her a heathen. To say "I don't know who God is" or "I've never held His hand" might burst their fragile bubble of companionship, and then she'd have no mortar with which to build dreams.

The station's flag, waving from the flagpole, came into sight. Then the depot emerged from its chrysalis of shrubs. The incongruity of the walk lay with Nelson's leisurely pace and the swift passage of time. She willed time to stretch another hour, another day, but the more she wished, the faster time sped by.

"May I have your address, Sylene?" Nelson asked. "I would like to send a post now and then, if I may. Mother has taken quite a fancy to you." He grinned a boyish smile that caused Sylene's pulse to jump skittishly, sending her mind down a path hemmed by hope on one side and despair on the other.

"We get our mail General Delivery at Bruceville. I would be pleased to hear from—either of you."

The coach had arrived. Passengers came and went in a blur, the loading and unloading happening too fast. "The driver won't tarry long," Nelson said. "I will see you aboard." Still holding her hand, he led her to the waiting transport. "We will meet again." Their eyes met, and it seemed to Sylene that their souls met. She could hear the heavy pounding of her own heart. "God go with you, dear."

Dear. Had he meant it, or did he use the endearment out of habit?

She was on the coach. The door closed, separating them. He turned about and was gone.

Sylene again sat by the window, a dull pain settling around her heart, and for an hour she watched the moving pictures of light without seeing. The mildew of misery tainted even the sunshine that filtered through to her. She would join her parents in Fort Worth, they would accomplish their shopping, and she would return to . . . to what? For a whole day, for twenty-four hours, she had been free from the Shadow, had found a place where she felt love and acceptance. It was another world, another sphere. It was like nourishment to a starving child.

Now the Shadow leapt back, shading her thoughts. She was ashamed of her feelings, yet she wished with all of her heart that she might escape the meeting with her parents and circumvent the acid of her mother's tongue. The sight of Sylene, a day late, could be the needle that lanced the boil of Trudy's ire, releasing the putrid bile of her choler.

Apprehension grew as the city's skyline emerged in the distance. Sylene wished she knew where to find God's hand. She looked at her own. Had Nelson really held it?

Had he really called her "dear"? He would probably forget to write, and she would likely never see him again. She must not feed her hopes.

The Fort Worth terminal was a large, modern building with oak paneling and polished floors. A refreshment stand occupied one end. People milled about, coming and going, the crowd so thick that Sylene could scarcely push her way through it. Had everyone in the city turned out to meet the coach?

Sylene's eyes, clouded by fright, scanned the mass of faces for Trudy and Evart. She went from one end of the station to the other and back again. But her parents were nowhere to be found.

CHAPTER Six

The Dress

"Pardon me, sir. I am looking for a Mr. and Mrs. Briggs."

The ticket agent's heavy, black brows creased. "Where would they have been routing, miss?"

"They came in from Bruceville yesterday on the eastern coach."

The big man pondered the matter. "A coach left going south about an hour ago, miss. I pride myself on my memory, and there *was* a man and woman who left on that car."

"Did she . . . did the lady have on a brown dress with a white collar?"

"It seems so. They were sitting when I came to work this morning. I suppose they slept right here. The poor dear wasn't any too happy. Her fret seemed to center on someone named Ann Marie. I wasn't eavesdropping, truly. She was just speaking rather loudly. Does that give you a clue?"

"Yes, sir. That would have been Mrs. Briggs. Ann

Marie is her daughter. I . . . I was supposed to meet them here, but I suffered a delay myself."

"I'm sorry." His dark eyes, so deeply set that they might have been peering from another world, rested on her with genuine sympathy.

"When . . . when will the next coach go toward Bruceville?"

"There won't be another coach going that direction until the day after tomorrow. We don't run on Sundays."

"Thank you, sir."

For a moment, Sylene stood motionless, paralyzed by indecision. Her heart wanted to run back to the Curtises. But she couldn't. Even if a tram ran to their door, she could not return. Nelson was there, and even though he had befriended her, even if he should love her, he would eventually discover the Shadow. The awful Shadow would build a wall between them, shading any attachment that might develop. With the Shadow she could go nowhere, build nothing. She could not take root or grow. It was like being half alive—or half dead.

She had no choice but to await Monday's coach to return to an angry mother, a mother who invested scant interest in her life or in her future. Turbulent emotions swirled within Sylene, wrestling savagely against her dark tomorrow. Was all of life but a dull and dreary journey, where one struggled through a fog and made no progress?

Minutes passed, and in the secret chambers of Sylene's heart, she gave a piteous cry for help. *God! If You are in Your heaven, help me!*

My child! It was a voice within her, and though it spoke only in her mind, she heard it. She looked up as if the voice came from the ceiling. Then, in a rush, Nelson's voice reading the Bible came back clearly: "Come unto me, all ye that labour and are heavy laden. . . ."

Her mind responded. *Here I am, God. I have come to You. I need direction.*

The ticket agent was back. "Miss, there is a nice and safe boardinghouse six blocks down the street that-a-way," he jerked his thumb to the north, "just past the Ladies' Shoppe. You can stay there until the coach comes through on Monday."

"I—"

"For a single person, it won't be more than a sawbuck for a couple of nights. To stay here until Monday would be much too wearisome. Do you have that much money in your handbag there? If you don't, I—"

Sylene had forgotten about the purse on her arm. "I . . . I think I do. I'll see." She opened the purse and found the thirty-eight dollars left from the purchase of the tickets. "Yes, sir, I have it."

Trudy would punish her for spending any of the money, but she could not sit here without rest or nourishment for forty-eight hours. Thanking the agent, she gathered her skirts and hurried from the building.

Along the street toward the large buildings of the city, horses napped at hitching posts. Three women had stopped to gossip in front of a general store; a lone man clumped along the wooden sidewalk to disappear into a saloon. Sylene hastened her pace.

Then she saw the dress.

Trussed on a wooden form in the window of a tiny establishment was the most beautiful garment Sylene had ever seen, as blue as a duck egg. A fitted bodice, wide sash, and delicately puffed sleeves lent elegance to the graceful flow of the skirt. There were dainty ruffles of lace at the wrists and the throat. She couldn't take her eyes from the lovely vesture, not realizing she had stopped stock-still to gaze upon it.

"Hello."

Sylene started.

"A lofly dress, no?"

"Y . . . yes."

"I feeneeshed the feengervork but this velly morning. I vill haff a sale for eet soon. Vould you be eenterested in trying eet on?"

"No, I—"

"There ees no harm een sleeping eet on, my dear. I am so velly anxious to see my handivork on somevun. Please do model eet for me! Come on een, and haff a cup of tea. Yes, please humor me. I am a beet egoteestical about my vork, I fear, and you are a just right size—" She had moved to Sylene's side, guiding her toward the door. "Oh, oh, I shall be so delighted to see how eet feets a real person!"

Sylene found herself inside the portals of a rose-scented room garnished with a wire-legged, white-topped table surrounded by gleaming old mirrors. "Here, dear." The proprietress was removing the dress from its stand. "Oh, vat a grand and glorious occasion!"

She helped Sylene remove her drab, homespun dress and deftly settled the blue dress over her shoulders. Then she fussed over each tiny button, tied the sash with a pat, and turned the girl toward the looking glass.

"See? Perfect! Vy, the pattern vas made just for you! See the nice feet? Just look! Your figure that asks no aid is carried, not made, by the lines of my vell-cut gown. Ah, dear, you haff the femineenity that creeps upon man's unvitting senses and enslaves him; he knows not how or ven or vy. And the exact match for your eyes! Amazing!"

Sylene had never considered herself a pretty lass. She continued standing in front of the mirror, looking hard, for perhaps the first time in her life, at the reflection which faced her. Until now, she had not "seen" her own beauty. The sight surprised her, set her heart to racing. She liked what she saw.

"I could make you a velly good deal on the garment," the saleswoman pressed. "Eef you vill purchase eet today, that ees. I alvays run specials on Saturdays so that my customers may look their best on the Lord's Day."

"Oh, I . . . I couldn't."

"You haven't the money?"

"Yes, I have the money, but without my mother's approval . . . I mean . . . well, you see, we came to Fort Worth to buy a dress for me. But—"

"Vonderful! Vy, eeny mother vould be glad for her daughter to own one of my creations! Yards and yards of the most eexpensive materials goes een the making. See that sign?" She pointed to the gold and black placard swinging from an iron post beside the door. It said simply *Marsha's*. "That name means a great deal to eferybody een Fort Vorth. I have a reputation for being the best seamstress een town. Eef your mother knows fashion, she vill be thrilled that you found thees dress before eet sold to somevun else."

"I don't think Mother would sanction anything so . . . so costly."

"I vill make you a good deal."

Sylene stood, stilled by an unreasoning reluctance to

change back into her faded cotton frock. "How . . . how much?"

"For eenybody else een the vorld, I vould charge seven dollars and feefty ceents. But the dress vas made for you. So for you only, the price ees seex dollars." The woman pursed her lips. "And I vill eenclude a seelk petticoat, some shoes, and a hair reebon."

Sylene calculated quickly. With five children in the Briggs family, her part would cover the six dollars. And since she was responsible for the benefit, shouldn't she be free to spend her portion as she chose? Surely her father would stand with her in the matter.

"Shall I box eet for you, or vill you wear eet?"

"I'll . . . yes, box it, please."

Surely the Shadow couldn't find her underneath the layers of rich fabric.

CHAPTER Seven

The Inn

The inn was on the left-hand side of the street. It stood three stories high. Round turrets rose at the four corners of the building, each topped by an ornately carved cupola. Windows as big as doors were framed by leaden panes of multicolored glass.

The innkeeper, who introduced himself as Mr. Arvilla, took Sylene's money, hardly glancing up when handing her a great skeleton key. "Upstairs. Second floor. Second door on the right. Supper at six. Breakfast at seven in the morning. Church service tomorrow at 9 A.M. in the great room. Have a pleasant stay." The inn, Sylene supposed, frequently served travelers stranded for the weekend.

In the clean and comfortable room, the strain of the past hours descended upon her in waves of nausea and a brutal, unrelenting headache. She was exhausted in soul and in body, wanting only to sleep, sleep and forget. Since leaving home, she had already made three unwise decisions: to allow herself to nap and miss her destination, to spend time with the Curtises, and to buy a dress that would serve no practical purpose in her life on the farm. She would pay dearly for each of her foolish blunders. But she'd deal with her mistakes later. Now she must rest, trusting that her head would stop its fierce throbbing. Stretched across the bed, she fell asleep, but it was not a restful sleep.

Faces peered at her, voices whispered, she was discovered or nearly discovered a dozen times, she crept away from following footsteps, she fell out of windows. In her final nightmare, her mother was coming for her purse. She would learn that Sylene had squandered money on a becoming dress and a sleeping room. Sylene must run for her life. Trudy was at the door—Sylene struggled to lock it. But there was no lock. Even the doorknob was gone, leaving the door to hang uselessly on its hinges.

Sylene fled from room to room, seeking escape. Behind her a chilling wind blew, the door banged rhythmically in time with the louder and louder sound of Trudy's steps. Trudy shouted threats, her voice rabid.

Sylene sat bolt upright. "I'm sorry, Mother! Please, forgive me! You and Father were not at the station!" At the sound of her own voice, she awakened fully. The room was dark. She had missed the evening meal.

She removed her clothing and, utterly spent, lay down again. But her mind stubbornly refused to quiet, replaying the visit to the Curtises, every minute of it from her first glimpse of Nelson to his parting words at the station, "We will meet again. God go with you." She squeezed her eyelids together to make the vision go away. Since she would not see Nelson again, she must forget.

At length, she fell into another fitful sleep, half awakening again and again with a sense of having narrowly escaped some terror which her dreams were about to reveal. Dawn finally came, and she welcomed the gray daylight that seeped through the windowpanes, warming them and settling over the room like mist. The smells of bubbling coffee and frying ham blended into a single, early morning fragrance, tantalizing her stomach. She was ravenously hungry.

Slowly she sat up, her eyes fixed upon the big box that lay beside the bed. Her dress. This was Sunday, and she would wear it. *Best wear it while you can,* the Shadow mocked, *for when you get home, Ann Marie will have it.*

The garment wouldn't look the same on Ann Marie. Ann Marie didn't have the height for it and wasn't quite past the days of flat immaturity. Her eyes weren't blue; they were green. But, of course, she would claim it anyhow. The Shadow was right. The echoing reminder was like turning the pages of an old photo album and finding the same picture on each page, a different name under each one.

Sylene tried to quell the unlovely thoughts. It was useless. The Shadow pierced the wall of forgetfulness that she'd tried so diligently to build, and when the barrier was weakened, the old confusion and abject helplessness wracked her heart anew.

Feelings Sylene had never quite laid bare surfaced. Trudy wanted Ann Marie to be happy but went to great efforts to destroy her eldest child's sense of well-being. There had to be a reason. What was Trudy's motive? Sylene knew she was on the verge of a revelation. Ann Marie, or rather her mother's favoritism to Ann Marie, was somehow connected with the Shadow. If she could find all the pieces to the puzzle . . .

The clock struck seven. Hunger hurried Sylene from the bed and to the washstand, furnished with an array of soaps, towels, and toiletries. She had never spent a night in a hotel, but she assumed these luxuries were placed in her room for her convenience. She would tell Ann Marie and Rosalind about all the niceties. No, she wouldn't. They would be envious . . .

Dressing carefully, Sylene pulled her bronze curls back with the ribbons. *If only Nelson could see me now!* Even as the unbidden thought came, she chopped it down. Why bother to hope? To dream? Wishful thinking had no place in her hapless existence.

All eyes turned toward Sylene as she entered the hotel's dining area. She heard a sharp intake of breath as she approached the table but disassociated it with her impact on the diners. "Sit anywhere you like, miss," the manager invited, "and enjoy your breakfast."

Two or three younger men scooted about to make a place for her, but she took her seat beside an elderly gentleman. "May I sit here, sir?" she asked.

"Certainly, certainly, milady!" he babbled. "My pleasure. Such a lovely creature my failing eyes have not beholden in a passel of fortnights. Be my guest. Be my guest." So eagerly did he pat the chair beside him that she wished she had chosen another location.

"And what enchanted isle do you hail from, and what brings you here to dine with us mere mortals?" he quizzed, a twinkle of mischief in his faded eyes.

"I'm from—" Something checked her. "I came in on the northbound stage on Friday and arrived here yesterday. I came to do a bit of shopping. I will be returning on the morrow."

"Oh, that's good. That's good. No, that's not good. I mean, it is good that you came, but it is not good that you will be going so soon. So soon." The man talked fast, substantiating his comments by repeating himself. "Surely you have had a successful journey. Your attire—I suppose it is new—is most lovely. Most lovely. It becomes you."

"Thank you, sir."

"My name is Felix. Felix Hermann. The first name is Felix and the last name is Hermann, though some folks get them mixed because Hermann does sound like a common first name. What is your name?"

"Sylene."

"A lovely name. A lovely name."

The waiter appeared with a heaping tray of flapjacks and warm syrup. "Your first course, ladies and gentlemen, from our marvelous chef. There is more to come!"

What she ate or how much, Sylene couldn't have told, for the old man beside her had begun his philosophizing.

"Such a bonny lass as yourself has a beau, I'm sure? I'm sure!"

"I . . . I don't plan to marry at all!"

Felix Hermann laughed, a deep guffaw. "That's what all girls in love say. You just gave yourself away. You are certainly in love."

Sylene fought feelings of dislike for the old man. In five minutes, he'd unearthed her secret. How should he know what railed in her heart, what abused her emotions?

"I say marriage is the sweet cure for love. If you cannot blot his face from your mind, if his mere glance makes your heart capsize in your chest, if you dream of him day and night—yes, day and night—I would strongly advise you to marry him."

"I . . . I don't plan to marry—"

Felix Hermann went right on, "There is a saying that no man has tasted the full flavor of life until he has known poverty, love, and war. Those three conditions embrace all there is in life worth remembering. Just don't try to crowd all three into a small space of time, my dear. Take them one at a time. One at a time."

"I—"

"All three experiences have beset me, and love has outlasted. I do the love of my life the favor of taking frequent and protracted trips. When I return, she welcomes me once again. In this way, our marriage has a good chance to last forever. Yes, forever. Now, tell me about this man you love."

"Really, sir, I only met him two days ago."

"Ah, it matters not. It matters not. Two days or two decades. If he has seized you by the heart, you will forgive him whatever his shortcomings. My dear lassie, women love nothing better than to forgive. This trait is so prevalent in their nature that some will attach themselves to rogues for the sheer pleasure of forgiving them indefinitely. It's so. It's so. Just ask my wife."

Sylene wanted to hear no more and was abruptly saved by Mr. Arvilla's presence at her elbow. "We have a little church service each Lord's Day, miss. We hope that you will join us."

"I would be delighted," Sylene said, arising and pushing back her chair.

"Each Sunday we have a visiting preacher. Today it

will be Brother Sams from over at Burleson. He is one of our favorites."

"Pleased to have met you, milady. Pleased to have met you," Mr. Hermann said, extending his leathery hand. "I'm not a churchy person, so I'll be going for my nap. We'll meet again at dinner, okay?"

The old-timer hurried away.

"Don't let the old gentleman bother you with his prattle, Miss Briggs," Mr. Arvilla suggested. "He comes here every weekend, out of sheer loneliness, I suspect. He loves being around other people. He has a good heart, really."

CHAPTER Eight

The Clock Salesman

On Sundays the inn's great room was converted into a chapel. A wooden podium stood on a dais, center front, with rows of chairs for the attendees. Sylene took her place near the back, inconspicuously tucking her full skirt about her legs so as not to encroach on the space of others.

About twenty people attended the service (Sylene's estimate), she being the youngest. She had never been to a church service and marveled that she did not feel out of place. Rather, she embraced a sense of belonging. As the congregation sang, she followed in the hymnbook, her voice blending with the others.

Looking back on the sermon, she wondered if God had designed the lesson especially for her. Not that she was worthy of special attention, she reminded herself, but it seemed that she gleaned more than her share of enlightenment from Brother Sams's candid message.

He taught on "The Will, the Heirs, and the Inheritance." Sylene listened with intense concentration. A legal will, Brother Sams pointed out, was immutable. When one received property, money, or a special endowment as a bequest, the heir had exclusive rights to that commodity's benefits and disposition. No other person had a right to dispute, claim, or disburse it.

For instance, Brother Sams expounded, if his grandmother left him a hundred dollars in her will, the money would be his to do with as he chose. He would have no obligation to share with aunts, uncles, or cousins. Grandmother meant for him to enjoy her gift.

Then he made the spiritual application. Christ left a will for mankind, he explained, so that each of us might receive the promise of an eternal inheritance, as the apostle mentioned in the Book of Hebrews. "We are God's heirs," the preacher said. "When our Savior died on Calvary, He made provisions in His will to care for our needs. There is healing in His will. There is salvation in His will. He arose from the grave to see that the conditions of His will are properly administered. No one can take our righteousness, our peace, or our joy from us, for these are included in our rich inheritance. If we do not accept them, the loss is ours, and the One who willed them to us will be disappointed.

"The devil would like to take away our inheritance," continued Brother Sams, "but we dare not allow that to happen. We must not give him even a part of our endowment, for God gave it to us that we might have a better life: eternal life. Who will accept God's gift and cherish it?"

Sylene didn't remember kneeling. All she remembered was the bitterness melting and the peace flowing in. Not in a rush of illumination, of sudden light, nor in a noisy demonstration. Rather, a hand touched her shoulder, and

God welcomed her in infinite tenderness into His kingdom. *Sylene, My child . . . My daughter . . . My heir.*

Crying broke forth like a child's wail for breath at the time of his birth. Words that she did not understand came forth from the center of her being. She didn't know what happened or how it happened—but she was changed. And she knew she would never again be the same.

She rose to her feet, her eyes closed against the unfamiliarity that lay at the quick of the usual world. "I have been saved," she whispered, probing her roused consciousness, testing the returning life of her senses, awed by the wonder of this miracle that had happened. "Yes, I have been saved."

Back in her room, Sylene pondered the things that the preacher had said. According to him, the money that Mrs. Oakum left to her belonged to her and to no one else. She was within her rights when she had bought the dress, a dress that was appropriate for her to wear to God's house. Dear Mrs. Oakum would be disappointed if her heiress did not keep the money and enjoy it. To divide the gift between her siblings or anyone else would be dishonoring the deceased lady's wishes, defeating her purpose in the bestowal. She would keep the gift.

Trudy would be livid and might even threaten to turn Sylene out, but Sylene must explain her position and stand her ground—for Mrs. Oakum's sake. Tomorrow she would return to her home and settle the issue . . .

For the rest of the day, Sylene was like a child clothed with a new garment, who stroked it with a tentative finger, seeking to understand its texture, admiring its colors. She wished that she had a Bible to read, hungering for more insight.

At dinner, she tried to avoid Mr. Hermann, but he came to sit beside her. "I hope that you enjoyed your church as much as I enjoyed my nap," he chattered.

"I enjoyed it very much, sir," she said. "I was saved."

"Humph," he muttered. "Won't be long before someone comes along to *un*save you. There's too much black in the world for one to stay white. Time smudges all of us. Yep, time smudges."

"The preacher said that Christ provided for our keeping in His will, sir."

"Have it your way, milady. Have it your way. And pray for this old, sinful man."

"I will, sir." Great compassion fell upon Sylene's soul. Here was a man who needed salvation. Though she had not understood what had happened, she had just received her first assignment in the new kingdom.

During the night, the rain began, a steady downpour. By morning, the street was pocked with brown puddles ankle deep. Women with umbrellas picked their way through the mud to the general store to buy their supplies.

"The coach won't run in this weather," piped old Mr. Hermann at breakfast. "Nope, not in this weather. You might as well plan to stay put, milady. Might as well stay put. And the same for me, but my wife won't mind. She'll get another scarf embroidered or another doily crocheted."

Another day at the inn would cost money. However, since Sylene had concluded that it was her money, every cent of it, she felt better. Whatever she spent, there would be no apologies to make to her mother. If she wished to stay a week or a month, the privilege was hers. Her absence from the home would be welcomed; only the money in the purse would be missed.

It rained dawn and day and dusk and did not abate the next day. Or the next. On Wednesday, the housekeeper was called away to attend to an ill family member, and Mr. Arvilla asked Sylene if she would like to work a few hours a day for her keep. Her uniform would be provided. She accepted the job, promising assistance until the maid returned.

With busy hands, Sylene suffered no homesickness. She was among people whose wants she could fulfill and who expressed their gratitude for the extra care she gave them. With much attention and very little system, she marshaled them through each day, changing linens, ironing pillow slips, filling pitchers, sweeping, and dusting. Hers was a job that she understood. The faster her feet moved, the more peaceful her mind. If a hotel guest had holes in his socks, Sylene mended them. She heated milk for children.

"Sylene, you must slow down!" laughed Mr. Arvilla. "You are spoiling our guests!"

Mr. Hermann went home but was back by week's end. "I can't stand all that quilt piecing," he said. "And the food is better here. Yep, things are better here. This place is my little private sun, milady. Each of us has a warm place for his soul to bask in: some dream, some hobby, some hope, which—though perhaps starving to nothing—lives on, as hope will. This is my cozy place. Yep, this is it."

He focused his watery eyes on Sylene. "But let me tell you, milady, with all this pampering, some young man is going to forget his manners and seek your hand."

"You have no worries, Mr. Hermann," assured Sylene.

But a clock salesman proved the old man right. He registered at the inn for a week's stay. Gilling was a young man who strutted when he walked and dressed in vogue. His fast gait invariably slowed when he neared Sylene. He ogled her throughout the meals and followed her to the kitchen where he cornered her. "Miss Briggs," he effused without parlay or preface, "do you go out much?"

Sylene drew back, but he went on, outlining ways he could deliver her from boredom. To begin with, there was a symphony at the concert hall that night.

Sylene washed dishes in frantic haste.

"How about it? Do you like music?" Gilling probed.

Sylene loved music, but she didn't like the man's boldness. "Yes, but I—"

"Then I'll get tickets for us."

Even Sylene's icy silence scarcely served to check him. It was the devil's instant for approaching the girl. She had no confidante, no counselor. That was the most opportune moment for a man like Gilling. Though craving and needing a companion at this hour of her life, she did not want Gilling to be the one.

"No," she said, and that was all that she could think of.

"What's the matter? Won't the boss let you off? Come, what is this place to you? There's a big world full of things to see and do! We'll be married, we'll travel, we'll see the world. You shall know what love can mean and what life really is. Miss Briggs, dearest—"

"*No!*"

Felix Hermann appeared in the doorway. "Sir, we are very busy just now. Mr. Arvilla is very strict. I'm afraid Sylene will have to refuse your kind invitation."

"Scared of your boss and scared of a good time,"

countered the salesman, strutting from the room. "Die in the dishpan then!"

"Thank you," Sylene whispered to Felix. "I . . . I didn't know what to say to a . . . a customer."

"You are not obligated to the customers here. Remember that, milady. I will report the man to Mr. Arvilla. I can smell these rats a mile away. If I mistake not, the man has a wife, but he doesn't wear a button portrait of her on his lapel. Ah, yes, he's vaguely conscious of her and even listens to her conversation sometimes. He knows she'll have a nice dinner for him when he comes home. But away from his home, he is a sport."

"He didn't do anything . . . bad."

"Nevertheless, he needs to be taught a thing or two." The old gentleman's eyes sparkled with impish delight. "I'm going to the parlor to tell him you'll go to that concert with him tonight."

"I . . . I couldn't do that—"

Mr. Hermann held up a shaking finger. "I'll tell him you didn't accept before because your mean, old boss wouldn't approve."

"But, sir—!"

"I'll tell him you'll sneak out."

"But I don't want to go out with him!"

"You aren't going with him. But when he calls your name under the window tonight, put your head out the shutters and answer him."

"What are you going to do?"

"Young men with pride like that one have to be spilled hard, milady."

Mr. Hermann's plan was totally successful. When the salesman appeared out of the darkness beneath Sylene's window, the old gentleman, with deadly accuracy, dumped cold water over him from an upper story, laughing all the while. "I guess he'll leave milady alone after this," Felix said the next morning.

"He wasn't really bad," was her only comment, remembering the dark eyed young man who was cocky and bragging when dry, but helpless and pathetic when soaked. Who knew what another's lot in life might be? "What if he catches cold and can't sell his clocks?"

"Women!" sighed the old man, "You're just like my wife! She fussed about the rabbit in her garden that ate her vegetables, and when I shot the rabbit, she was mad at *me*!"

CHAPTER Nine

Nelson's Visit

When Trudy Briggs learned at the Bruceville depot that Sylene had taken her purse, she worked herself into a frenzy. "If it were just the money, Evart," she cried, "I could bear it. But my papers are in the purse! I have guarded those papers carefully ever since Sylene was born; they are more important to us than anything else in the world. They are our future!"

There was much that Evart didn't know; Trudy had misguided his thinking throughout their marriage. He thought that Trudy's first husband was dead—which was not true. He believed that he married a poor struggling widow left with a newborn baby—which was not true. He made allowances for her "moods" because of the tragedies that he supposed she had suffered. He knew about the insurance money that was coming on Sylene's eighteenth birthday and hoped that the fortune might make his own life more pleasant. Many times he had wished himself beyond the reach of Trudy's acrid tongue, but he did not believe in divorce. He married for better or for worse and had been cursed with the worst.

"You must find Sylene, Evart. She has stolen my purse and run away. I think she snatched the purse when I wasn't looking."

"The agent said the purse was left laying and that he flagged the coach to get it to Sylene."

"Agents will say anything if you slip them a bit of money. Sylene paid him to tell us that! Now, find her and get my purse back!"

"We haven't the money for another trip."

"Sell one of the cows."

Evart left on Wednesday, and a letter came for Sylene on Thursday's post. Ann Marie helped herself to the opening of it. "It is from a boy, Mama!" she yelled. "Sylene has found a beau."

Trudy jerked the page unceremoniously from Ann Marie's hand and read it aloud:

My dear Sylene,

I hope that you made your trip to the Fort Worth station and met your family with no problems. Mother and I miss you dreadfully. Mother is fine; she mentions you often. I will be traveling to Fort Worth myself in a few weeks to keep an appointment. In the meantime, I would like to call on you if I may. Please consult your parents and see if it will be okay with them for me to visit you in your home. May I hear from you?

Your new friend,
Nelson Curtis

"See, Mama! I should have been the one to go to Fort Worth first; then I should have met this Nelson fellow. He sounds like a treat." Ann Marie stopped abruptly and tossed her head. "But it isn't too late. *I'll* answer the letter. I'll invite him to visit. When he sees me, he will forget all about Sylene. Sylene stole our money, so I'll steal her boyfriend. Just you wait and see. And it will serve her right!"

Trudy laughed. "You've always been the clever one, Ann Marie. No young man can resist your charm. I dare say you'll win, and Sylene will have her desserts. I've considered the problem, and I'm not much worried about Evart finding her. She'll come home broke, hungry, and beggarly before her eighteenth birthday."

"And beau-less!"

Ann Marie didn't squander a day in responding to Nelson's letter. She wrote that although Sylene was not at home at present, the family expected her to arrive any time. Her sister, she wrote, as well as the rest of the family, would enjoy his call. Drawing a map that directed him to the farm, she delivered the message to the post personally, giving herself accolades all the way there. Any young man who gave Sylene attention would give her "more attractive" sister more attention.

The following week Nelson came, bearing a massive sheaf of flowers. Ann Marie met him at the door with ostentatious fanfare. "Please, do come in, sir!"

"I am Nelson Curtis, a friend of Sylene's. If I may see her, please?"

"I'm afraid she isn't here today, sir. I am her sister, Ann Marie, and I'm pleased to meet you, I'm sure." She batted her eyelashes.

"Will Sylene be in soon?"

"We have not heard from my sister, sir, since she was separated from our parents on a trip to Fort Worth—"

"Oh, I do hope that nothing has happened! I should have accompanied her to Fort Worth myself. I have berated myself for not doing so." Alarm registered in his eyes.

"Oh, I'm sure she is all right, sir. She is most capable of caring for herself. Since she was fifteen, she has been quite independent, working away from home for days at a time. We really aren't worried for her safety. If only she would be responsible enough to write home and let us know her whereabouts!"

"When I saw her to the coach in Cleburne, she was planning a reunion with her parents and an immediate trip home."

"Who knows about Sylene? She is a flighty one. She may have met up with some old friend—" Ann Marie paused. "But now that you are here, please visit awhile. Let's become better acquainted."

Ann Marie was too self-conscious to notice Nelson's efforts to conceal his bitter disappointment. He suddenly became aware of the bouquet he held in his hands, trying to decide what to do with it.

"The flowers are gorgeous!" burbled Ann Marie.

"I guess since Sylene is not here, I shall give them to you or your family."

"Oh, thank you!" gushed Ann Marie. "They are the loveliest flowers I have ever seen! Truly, they are." She held them to her lips, a trick to draw his focus to their sensuous pucker. Then she let one eyelid drop. "I love flowers, which makes me just a little glad that Sylene is not here."

Trudy appeared, all spurious smiles, to support Ann Marie in insisting that Nelson stay for dinner. "You must be hungry," she coaxed. "We will be most delighted to have you as a guest at our meal."

Windsor and Chuckie exhibited their best behavior, while Rosalind fluttered about with the serving. They'd been trained to please Ann Marie, who sat primly beside Nelson, chatting companionably.

"Sylene and I met at the Cleburne station," Nelson volunteered, "and she spent a day in our home. I found her to be a gracious young lady. I'm afraid she stole my mother's heart, as well as—"

Trudy grew bold. "Yes, Sylene makes a good first impression," she agreed. "But she has been a rather difficult child, I must say. I never know what she will do next. She is quite capricious. Now, Ann Marie and Rosalind have never given a minute's trouble in their lives." She craftily steered the conversation away from Sylene, flinging Ann Marie into Nelson's thoughts at every opportunity.

Nelson favored Ann Marie with a dazzling smile. "I hope that you will let me know when your sister returns."

"My pleasure."

After the repast, Trudy suggested that Ann Marie show Nelson around "the place." "The farm isn't much," she lamented. "It is but leased. However, we plan to buy a nice ranch before the year ends. We've been working toward that goal for many years. My husband has promised me new appointments for the house, as well as a surrey."

That Nelson's mind was occupied elsewhere did not cross Ann Marie's self-centered mind. As they toured the grounds, she gabbed about the henhouse, the barn, the fields, and the horses. Surely no one could be more interesting or desirable than herself, she thought. But when they had walked about for a while, he asked pointedly, "Do you think there is a chance that Sylene will return today?"

Ann Marie tossed her head. "I don't know. Mama thinks she may have decided to run away and get married. She took . . . some of our savings when she left. I really don't expect her ever to come back."

"Then I will be going," he said abruptly. "I came to talk with her about . . . about our future, and if there is none—"

Realizing her mistake, Ann Marie backtracked quickly. "Oh, she might be back at any time, of course. Perhaps you would like to wait? Or come again another day?" She laid a hand on his arm.

"Please tell her to send me a note when she gets home—if she would like to see me."

Ann Marie knew that she had lost his attention, but she didn't know how or where. None of her frantic efforts recaptured it. "I hope you will write to her again soon."

Nelson was gone.

But Ann Marie had his address. She would not let this prize slip between her fingers. If she had to pursue him, she would do so.

"Ooh! He is handsome," cooed Rosalind. "I can't imagine why he would be interested in Sylene."

"That was before he met me," Ann Marie quipped. "The next time he comes, I will have some eye shading and face paint. And some red nail polish. That wins them every time."

CHAPTER Ten

The Convert

As the days after her conversion came and went, Sylene found that life was the same. And yet it wasn't. It went on, certainly, work and rest, sunlight and darkness, fair days and gray ones. The spring storms ceased, and deep summer settled over the city.

There were problems just as there had been before, and sometimes it seemed that there were more now than ever. Or perhaps she was more aware of other people, of their grief and their joy; and their cares multiplied her own. But her face was set in another direction now. She seldom thought of Nelson.

Another week passed. And yet another. The maid sent word that she would be absent yet longer. The doctor had pronounced her relative terminally ill, and she would nurse her to the end.

Sylene eagerly looked forward to the Sunday services. Her one good dress was meticulously preserved for these special occasions. She hoped that Brother Sams would keep coming to preach, but he could not. The next preacher was a Brother Wentworth, who half read and half quoted from memory his sermon in a vigorous voice that demanded rapt attention. "For out of the heart proceed evil thoughts, murders, adulteries, fornications, thefts, false witness, blasphemies."

Sylene carefully checked the list of sins as the preacher intoned. *Then I'm no sinner . . .*

"So you think you're not a sinner?" Brother Wentworth blurted as if he'd read her thoughts.

Sylene jumped.

"Well, listen to this."

Sylene leaned forward to listen.

"But I say unto you, That whosoever is angry with his brother—"

Sylene heard no more of the service. The door of her memory burst open, and she was too weak to close it. She had been angry with Ann Marie. With Rosalind. With her mother. Her heart seethed with rancor. She must expunge the iniquity. As the service swept into the brisk cadences of its conclusion, she stood with the rest of the congregation, but her soul was on its knees seeking forgiveness. Oh, she had so much to learn!

With the anger conquered, Sylene felt better. Now she had cleaned her spiritual house, swept and mopped it. It was ready for God's inspection.

For the next service, she dressed with particular care, coiling her hair atop her head, fencing it about with the blue ribbon. The beveled mirror in her room threw back a good reflection, accentuating her sapphire eyes. Though her happiness wasn't complete, she was as near to that attribute as she had ever been—and she was probably as close as she would ever be, she conceded.

The front seat of the chapel was her preference for the services now, as she hoped to absorb every grain of soul food. The preacher was late this day, and she had her eyes closed with the fervency of her worship when he walked in. She looked—and looked again. The evangelist was none other than Nelson Curtis. He glanced over the audience, but he did not recognize her.

She had forgotten how handsome he was, how the dark lock of hair fell over his forehead, and how he affected her heart. It had taken her days to forget, and in seconds, all the enamored feelings came flooding back, breaking the dam of her resistance.

Since he did not recognize her, his ministering would not be affected by their past acquaintance. She was glad of that. But it almost proved her undoing when he read the scripture, *her* scripture: "Come unto me, all ye that labour and are heavy laden, and I will give you rest." Tears pooled in her eyes.

"There are rooms here in the inn," Nelson said, "where one can rest from his earthly journey. But God also has 'rooms' of rest in His kingdom. There is a room of righteousness, a room of peace, and a room of joy in the Holy Ghost." Then he talked about baptism, which washed away one's sins. One could not truly "rest" until his sins were covered by the covenant of baptism. Baptism was the burial of one's past so that, thereafter, one might walk in newness of life.

Sylene knew nothing about baptism; the message was new to her. She had not been baptized, and if this was a step of salvation, she needed to take it. But how? And where?

After the service, she approached Nelson. "Sir," she said, "I would like to be baptized."

Nelson stared at her as if trying to dredge up a long lost memory. "Of course, ma'am. I am sure that we can arrange that. When—?"

"As soon as possible."

"How about today? A pond is nearby. You might like to go home to change your clothes—"

"Yes, I will do that. That is, I live here. I work here."

Nelson studied her face closely. "Pardon me for staring, but you look very much like a young lady I know, a . . . a dear friend of mine. But there is a . . . a difference . . ."

Sylene smiled. "I hope that is a compliment."

"It was meant to be, for sure."

"Perhaps I shall meet your friend someday."

"I hope that I may locate her. I have—lost track of her. Would after lunch be a good time—for the baptism, I mean?"

"Yes, sir. Whenever it is convenient for you. I thought that I had been saved recently, but after hearing your sermon, I know that I need to be buried with Christ in baptism. I want my sins covered."

"Absolutely."

Sylene settled herself at the far end of the table from Nelson at lunchtime. She didn't trust herself to sit nearer. Nelson sat, unfortunately, by Felix Hermann.

"Are you married, young man?" Mr. Hermann pried loudly.

"No, sir."

"How old are you?"

"I will be twenty-three on my next birthday."

"I was married when I was thirty, young man. I should

have wed at a younger age. By thirty, one gets set in one's ways. But I wasn't a parson, you see. A parson needs a helpmeet to coddle the lady folk. It's hardly befitting for a man to coddle them, now is it? Have you ever thought on a wife?"

"Yes, sir."

"Do you already have one in mind?"

"Yes, sir."

"Well, whoever she may be, you couldn't best our little housekeeper here." He lowered his voice, but being hard of hearing himself, he didn't realize that everybody at the table could hear even the lesser volume. "'Tis that lovely girl at yon end of the table in the blue dress. Yep. She's the closest thing to an angel I ever glimpsed. The closest thing."

"She has asked that I baptize her today, sir."

"She? If she's bad enough to need a baptizing, I reckon I need to be baptized forty times save one. I'm just an old sinner—according to my wife, anyhow—but if you baptize her, would you baptize me, too? Could you baptize me?"

"Do you believe in the death, burial, and resurrection of Jesus?"

"Sir, whatsoever that little lady yonder believes, I believe. She's nothing but pure good. Nothing but good."

The baptism was set for two o'clock. Nelson borrowed some trousers from Mr. Arvilla. He waited in the lobby for the candidates. When Sylene came downstairs in her feed sack dress, Nelson took a step backward, stumbled on a cuspidor, and fell headlong into a chair. "Sylene!" he cried, righting himself. "It is you! Why, I didn't even recognize you in that fancy frock."

Felix Hermann waddled in, missing the excitement. "I'm ready, parson," he remarked. Then he turned to Sylene. "It's a pity, lass, that this goodly, young preacher man already has his heart set on a bride. I like him. Yep, I like him. You and he would sure have made a smart match! Yep, a smart match."

Nelson gave Sylene a mischievous wink.

CHAPTER Eleven

The Promise

"Do you have time to visit awhile, Sylene?" Nelson asked. "If it wasn't the Lord's Day, I would take you for a soda. But the drugstores aren't open on Sundays, and that blue law is an honorable rule."

Sylene had changed back into her blue dress, pulled her wet hair into a tight knot which lay heavily lustrous against the demure neckband of the bodice, and sat in the hotel's parlor, feeling clean inside and out. Nelson's nearness brought a warm rush of blood, a new and strange emotion, causing elation and a greed for the future. It was a curious sensation. Perhaps this was what people meant by happiness. She wished it might never end.

"I have a lot to tell you," he began.

To Sylene's chagrin the old-timer chose this time to hobble in. "Well, now, I hope that in your little chat, sir, you plumb forget that other woman you are so set on. Yep, plumb forget. This one here is a queen. If I were a young man and was choosing again, I'd dibs on her. I sure would. But I'll be going along to my nap now so that you two can talk." He limped out, turning to say, "Thank you for the baptizing. I feel mighty good. Thank you."

"There's your first convert," Nelson grinned.

"I don't know what I did—"

"It isn't so much what we do as what we are. Mr. Hermann saw Christ in you, and he wants to be like you. God has counted you worthy to fulfill all the good pleasure of His righteousness, and the name of our Lord Jesus Christ is being glorified in you. It is a wonderful calling, Sylene. You are doing a fine job."

"I . . . I hope so. I'm just starting to learn about God. I'm still in the first grade!" Sylene said. "I don't even have a Bible."

"We'll have to fix that."

"Yes, I plan to buy one next week."

"I wanted to tell you that I met your family."

"My . . . family?" Sylene tried to hide her surprise. "Were they . . . well?"

"They were. In fact, your mother was quite beside herself over the prospect of the new farm."

"The new farm?"

"You didn't know about it?"

"No, sir."

"Your mother tells me that they are purchasing a ranch with a nice home in a couple of months. She's eager to have lovely furnishings and a carriage."

"I can't imagine where they will get the money to buy a ranch. We've always rented and have never had the funds for a down payment."

"She was very positive about it."

"I hope that she isn't disappointed. But . . . but where did you meet my family?"

"I went to Bruceville. I wrote to you, and your sister answered. She said they expected you home right away, and she invited me for a visit. I went."

"You met . . . Ann Marie?"

"Yes. I met all of your family except for your father. He was out searching for you. Or he was searching for your mother's purse, I believe. It seems they lost some important papers when they lost it."

"I have the purse, but I . . . I didn't know about the important papers. I did have some personal money in the purse—"

"I don't think they were concerned with anything but the papers."

"I had planned to return home at once. But the rain came, and then Mr. Arvilla asked me to help out for a few days when the housekeeper was called away. I have worked away from home before, and I didn't suppose that my parents would object."

"You are planning to return home soon?"

"Yes, I'll go when the regular maid comes back. Actually, I haven't felt it was the right time to return before now. I . . . I had to find God, and I've learned so much here."

"And now you can lead the rest of your family to God."

"I . . . I hope so."

"I will visit again when you are there. I hope that I might help with the winning of them. They responded to me well, especially Ann Marie."

"Ann Marie is sixteen, almost seventeen."

"Yes, and a beautiful young lady! She showed me about

the place and made me feel quite at home. Your mother said that she had always been a gracious and lovely daughter. That being the case, she shouldn't be far from the kingdom of God. I had taken a bouquet of flowers for you, but knowing they would wilt before I got back home, I gave them to your sister. She seemed delighted to have them! I'll bring a fresh bunch when I come again."

A vague and evasive pain pricked Sylene's consciousness. She recognized it: the old, familiar Shadow. Her soul stood alone in the cloud. She was on earth, yet no one could hear her mortal cry. It avalanched into a magnified assurance of impending doom. Parallel in her heart ran a hopeless despair and a sick dread. A friendship as precious to her as this could only end in a final and annihilating stroke. Ann Marie would have Nelson's affection, the one thing that Sylene yearned for. Ann Marie would stop at nothing to rob her of her treasure.

Nelson talked on, but Sylene wasn't hearing. Her mind hacked at her secret dream, hating that dream. She pictured Marie Antoinette on her way to the guillotine. Only she, Sylene Briggs, was the martyr and another Marie was leading her to the chopping block. This was the drama of love's end: tragedy, heartbreak, and the death of hope.

"I would like to stay with you longer," Nelson was saying, reaching for his hat, "but I have committed myself to speak to a small group in Benbrook this evening. May I please send you a Bible, my dear Sylene? Let it be a bond between us. It is the Bible that belonged to my beloved father. Shall I send it to Bruceville or here?"

To Bruceville? If Ann Marie had a crush on Nelson, anything that arrived at the Bruceville address would be claimed as her own.

"When will you be sending it?"

"Before the week is up."

"I will be here yet. Please send it to this address, and I will take very good care of it."

With a handclasp that lingered, he was gone.

CHAPTER Twelve

The Discovery

When Felix Hermann came the following weekend, he brought Sylene an oil lamp for her room. "You might want to spend some nights writing to that preacher man," he touted, his eyes bright beneath the shaggy white eyebrows. "Or mayhap you'd like to write a story. Now, love stories, I say, are not properly a matter for printing but something to be privately handled by the alienists and florists. But women do like them, editors say. Editors are wrong, of course. Women do not read love stories in magazines. They read recipes for cucumber lotion. Love stories are read by ten-year-old girls. Just make certain that your stories—or your letters—have living substance, milady."

Sylene's lips quivered on the edge of a smile. "Thank you, Mr. Hermann. I think I shall not need the lamp for writing. I would like to do some reading, though."

Since the old-timer's baptism, his attitude had improved. He seldom mentioned his wife now, but when he did, he spoke in terms of endearment. "A better woman never lived," he said once, which roused Sylene's wonder as to why he didn't stay home with her or bring her along with him now and then. Once she was on the verge of asking, but something arose to distract her.

The lamp proved of little use to Sylene, for when summer's late darkness settled over the inn, she took to her bed, spent from the day's work. She would have no need to write to Nelson; she was sure Ann Marie was taking care of that. She had received the Bible as he had promised, along with a hurried note. He had had a long letter from Ann Marie, he said, and he hoped to see them all soon. He had marked some scriptures that had proven strengthening to himself, and they would discuss them further when he came to Bruceville to help her convert her family. She found nothing in the letter to nurture her emaciated hope.

The Shadow came to harrow often now, camping in Sylene's room, refusing to budge. Joining forces with her enemy, the lamp sent gloomy fingers dancing on the walls.

Then, one night, the Shadow's focus seemed to center on her mother's black purse. What papers could be so important as to warrant her parents' concern? Yes, she could understand her mother's anxiety over the cash in the purse, but Nelson indicated that the papers—whatever they were—imposed a graver solicitude than Mrs. Oakum's money. How could that be possible?

So troubled were her thoughts that Sylene went for the purse, turned the bag bottom up, and spilled the contents on the bed. The money fell out first, then her coach ticket, a handkerchief with a tatted edging, a buttonhook, and a corked vial of cheap perfume. There were no papers. To make sure nothing remained, she ran her hand along the inside of the purse. That is when she heard the crackle of parchment. Something was hidden in the lining.

At one time, she observed, the lining had been ripped away and then basted back in place. She almost started to abandon the search, castigating herself for her curiosity. After all, what hid in her mother's purse was none of her business. Or was it? If it were an item that needed immediate attention—a debt, an application, a certificate—she should make every effort to return it to her family before its expiration date. In fact, she should have mailed the purse back before now. It did not belong to her. Only the money and the ticket were hers.

Returning the objects to the handbag, she set it on the bureau, put out the lamp, and went back to bed. Nothing could be done to rectify the matter at this late hour. She would see to it tomorrow.

But she could not sleep. A sixth sense told her that some action must be taken, and she would do well to learn what her obligation might be. How could she know what to do if she were not apprised of the papers' content or intent? She tossed and turned, tumbling her sheets into a frightful rumple.

After an hour of sleepless fidgeting, she arose and lighted the lamp once again. She would not rest until she had satisfied her mind concerning the documents in question.

She tore away the cloth lining of the purse and pulled out an envelope. The packet contained two yellowed sheets of paper. Moving closer to the lamp, which now seemed to sputter in protest, she studied them.

The first was a birth certificate. Sylvia Arlene, the document revealed, was born on September 2, 1880, to Trudy Bessanne (Jones) Oliver and Thomas Josiah Oliver. That was her own date of birth! Did that mean her mother had been married before to Thomas Josiah Oliver? Was she this child, Sylvia Arlene? Or had she a twin who died?

The lamp flickered, suddenly burned low, then flared, causing the eerie light to bring forth a startling exposure. The "Trudy" before "Bessanne (Jones) Oliver" had been added with the stroke of a thicker quill. The ink differed ever so slightly—and probably would not be detectable under any other light.

So unsettled was Sylene by the birth certificate that she did not take the time to study the attached paper, which appeared to be a detailed legal directive. Her mind begged the leisure to absorb one thing at a time.

The facts shouted that this child was herself and that she did not belong to Evart Briggs. He was not her father. Who was Thomas Josiah Oliver? Was Trudy Briggs her mother? With the duplicity on the affidavit, she had her doubts. She bore but a slight resemblance to Trudy, none to Evart. This then would explain Trudy's jealousy. Trudy wanted no affection between the man and the daughter who bore no relationship to him. The thought sickened Sylene.

Ann Marie, as well as the other children, belonged to Trudy Briggs. They belonged to Evart. It made sense now, the favoritism. One's own flesh and blood always takes precedence. She, Sylvia Arlene Oliver, was an intruder.

A large shadow of her shape rose upon the wall and ceiling. The lamp's flame gyrated demonically, brandishing its lack of care about her strait. In an instant, the essence of life had changed. The Shadow deepened, dark-ened, and struck viciously, as though she could feel it paint a blot upon her soul.

You don't even know who you are, Sylene Sylvia Arlene Oliver Briggs! Your own mother may have been a barmaid and your father a thief. Else why would your origin have been hidden from you, the records of your birth guarded in the bowels of a black purse?

So she had been cast upon Trudy Briggs, a stranger who had not really wanted her. She was an intrusion, thrown into the lap of someone who'd been forced to share her time, her life, and her family with a castaway. Small wonder that Trudy was resentful, bitter, and wel-comed Sylene's absences.

However, the sum and substance of the imbroglio was not coming together. Why was Trudy so desperate to get the birth certificate back into her possession? Was she afraid that Sylene would find it? Or were there other, more consequential reasons?

With a flash of inner comprehension, Sylene knew that since she had discovered the document, this woman, Trudy, would be her mother figure no more, but her enemy. Trudy had never loved her, never would. For a moment, Sylene saw the bare soul of this woman whom she had called mother, even as at that moment she saw her own soul; and between this which she saw and that which remained in her own bosom, she recognized little kinship.

On the stormy sea of young adulthood, where did this put her? Now, even if Nelson Curtis loved her, wished to marry her, preferred her above Ann Marie, she could not allow his devotion. The girl he loved would not be her real self. The person he adored would be another in her body, one whom neither he nor herself knew.

And what if there were children? They would never know who their mother really was. They would not know their grandparents or what ghosts might lurk in their ancestry. She could not subject another human to the mental tortures she endured.

When Nelson learned that she was not Sylene Briggs, he would look upon her as an impostor, a guilty woman in the guise of an innocent one. And he, a preacher of God's holy Word, was worthy of more than a deceiver. A satiric psalm she had read in sixth grade came to haunt her, embodied in the voice of the Shadow:

Behold, when thy face is made bare,
He that loved thee shall hate;
Thy face shall be no more fair
At the fall of thy fate.

Deep ran her meditation until she became weary with thinking, eroded by thinking, withered by thinking: *Who am I? Who are my parents? Where are they?*

Deadened by introspection, she lay across the bed and, in a few minutes, forgot existence, her face still wearing the pain spread there by the discovery of the document.

And the night marched on, unconcerned and indifferent, the night that had swallowed the remainder of her hope and was now digesting it.

CHAPTER Thirteen

Surprise Guest

The lamp had burned out when Sylene arose in the light of an ashy and gloomy dawn, a day when she would eat without knowing that she ate, drink without tasting, gaze at a world now indistinct and shadowy, full of the terrors of uncertainty. Bringing with her no knowledge of her history, doubting her parentage, questioning her own identity, she felt unprotected, unprepared for today—or tomorrow. She must now plod into the unknown. She felt that some evil harpy of the air had swooped down and borne her into the pathless sky or that the ocean had closed over her and left no trace.

She tried to read the Bible that Nelson had sent but found concentration arduous. He had marked Psalm 37:4, "Delight thyself also in the LORD; and he shall give thee the desires of thine heart."

The desires of her heart? Today she couldn't grasp King David's meaning. She had no material desires. She wanted nothing more than to know who she was. If she could know this, the Shadow could no longer wrack her. She would be beyond the Shadow. But how could she ever know?

While mopping the kitchen, she heard a man's voice asking for "Miss Sylene Briggs." She broke into a cold sweat; it was the voice of Evart Briggs. "I am her father," he told Mr. Arvilla, "and I have come for a visit. Sylene's mother wants to know that she is well."

"Pleased to meet you, I'm sure," welcomed the proprietor. "Your daughter is here. She is a good worker, and we're fortunate to have her just now. One of our employees had to take a leave of absence. You will find Sylene about the place pushing a flatiron or toting a scrub bucket. Make yourself at home."

He has come for the money, Sylene surmised. Then, *No, it is for the certificate.*

Not waiting for him to come to her, Sylene went to greet him. "You are looking for me?" she asked, unsmiling.

The nap of his hat was ruffled, a patch worn away at its brim where his thumb rubbed when taking it off. "Well . . . yes, Sylene. I was in town on a little business, and I thought I would drop by for a few minutes." He gripped the hat with nervous fingers. "A young man of your acquaintance, I believe Ann Marie calls him Nelson, told us of your whereabouts."

Sylene stood immobile.

"It is good to see you again." He fumbled for words. "I am glad to see that you are well. Your mother has been concerned about you."

"Please tell her that I am fine. I have a job here."

"I shall tell her. And do tell me about yourself and your

work here so that I may relay the news. The boys miss you dreadfully. Your boss said that you might take a few moments from work to visit—"

"There isn't much to tell, sir. One of Mr. Arvilla's workers was called away, and he asked me to fill in for her until she gets back."

"Trudy sent word that she hopes you will be home by your birthday in September."

"We shall see what the future holds, sir."

"Your mother is planning a great celebration."

"You may tell her that I went ahead and bought a dress for myself. We have chapel services here each Lord's Day, and I wear it."

"She will be glad, I am sure."

"I will send some of the money so that the other children may have new clothes, too."

"That won't be necessary, Sylene. We . . . will soon be doing very well." His eyes shifted.

"Is it true that you are buying a ranch?"

"Yes. We found a lovely ranch for five thousand dollars cash. We are very excited. But we will wait until you come home to take possession so that you may choose your own room. There will be a room for each of you. The place has a large upstairs with six bedrooms. Trudy is beside herself, and Ann Marie especially looks forward to a drawing room to welcome her suitor. The boys like the fishing pond. Life will be better for us . . . right away."

"But I don't understand how . . . where—?"

"How we could buy such an elaborate place?" Evart chuckled. "It's a long story. Trudy was left some money by a friend many years ago. Until now, it has been tied up in an estate, and she hadn't access to it. However, she was

95

notified a short while back that the funds will be released early this fall. She is counting the days."

"I see. I'm happy for you."

"But do show me around. I would like to see your room so that I may describe it to Trudy and Ann Marie and Rosalind. They will be green with envy. Ann Marie has dreamed of staying in an inn. To think that a daughter of ours works in such a lovely place!"

Flattered and fooled by Evart's glib words, Sylene led him up the stairs to her quarters. He looked about, then walked to the window. "This is wonderful, Sylene. I see that you are quite comfortable. Please stay on as long as you are needed, but ask your boss if you may have a few days off to celebrate your eighteenth birthday with your family. Surely he will not begrudge you that."

"I should think that my employment would be ended by then. I am only a temporary replacement."

"That is good. But wait," he cupped his hand to his ear, "didn't I hear the owner calling for you? Yes, I'm sure that I did. Run along quickly and see what he wants. I'll wait here for you."

Sylene fell for the trickery. Hurrying down the stairs in search of Mr. Arvilla, she found him working in the flower bed outside. "You called for me, sir?"

"No, Sylene, I didn't call you. I would not disturb your visit with your father. Please take your time and enjoy his company."

Puzzled, Sylene returned to her room only to find that Evart Briggs was not there.

Neither was the black purse.

He had taken it and fled . . .

CHAPTER Fourteen

Missing Papers

Ann Marie's mad infatuation with Nelson Curtis was the breath and life of her being. It enveloped her as a photosphere, blotting out any gloomy specters that would persist in their attempts to touch her—doubt, fear, or his fondness for Sylene. Her happiness now depended entirely on Nelson. She thought every line in the contour of his person the ultimate of masculine perfection.

Nelson had come and gone, again missing Sylene. The box of dipped chocolates that he had left for Sylene was claimed by Ann Marie without compunction. "He was too shy to give the candy to me," she told Trudy, "but he meant it for me all the time."

"You are right, darling," encouraged Trudy. "If Sylene will stay away a few days longer, you will have Nelson's heart completely. I see it happening! No one can resist your sorcery."

"I love him, Mama, and I will marry him!" vowed Ann Marie, hugging her knees through her bedclothes. "Ever since I first looked into his eyes, he has been the only man in the world for me. I want to be happier than anybody. I want all the things, the good things, there are in the world. I want to travel, to meet intelligent people, to hear music, and to give parties of my own in my own home."

"Of course you will marry Nelson," agreed her mother. "Sylene shall not have what rightfully belongs to you. I will see that history does not repeat itself."

"What do you mean by that, Mother?"

"I guess you're old enough to know, Ann Marie. My older sister stole the love of my life from me. He was kind. He was handsome. He was generous—"

"Just like Nelson!"

"And he commanded a goodly payroll. But my sister would have him—she, who did not love him as I! Oh, she claimed she did, but she didn't. She couldn't. When he married her, I thought that my heart would break. With time, I would have won him back. I have no doubts. But he was killed."

"Oh, Mama! Don't say it! It is too, too sad!"

"My sister had everything she wanted in life. Her husband left her well fixed. A lovely home. Pretty clothes. Money.

"But I will not let it happen to you, Ann Marie. Whatever I must do—or whatever you must do—we will win. You shall not suffer as I have suffered all these miserable years."

"Oh, thank you, Mama!"

"Ann Marie, you must start the minute Sylene gets home to turn her heart from the man you love. Say things that will make her dislike him and give him the cold shoulder when he tries to talk with her. When she arrives, tell her how much Nelson loves you. Tell her that his attention to her is but courtesy to a sister of his beloved. Tell her— oh, tell her all sorts of things, Ann Marie, to deflect her. If you can cause her to spurn him, you will have a victory because a man cannot abide spurning. Oh, that I had thought of this with my own sister! Or if I'd had a mother to advise me in heart strategy!"

"I will write to Sylene and tell her that Nelson and I plan to be married. And it will not be a lie, for I do plan to marry him."

"That is an excellent idea!"

"I'll hint at a Christmas wedding. We'll be in our new home by then?"

"Yes, we'll plan for a Christmas wedding."

Ann Marie began planning. Aloud. But before their conspiracy burgeoned, Evart came bounding in, a satisfied smile on his face. "I found her, Trudy, at the inn where Nelson Curtis said she would be. And here is your purse." With a melodramatic bow, he dropped it on her lap.

Trudy snatched at the satchel and jumped to her feet. "Evart Briggs! You got the papers! I cannot believe our good luck." She kissed his cheek. "But tell me how—?"

"It was simple enough. In fact, it was much easier than I thought it would be. With gentleness and soft talk—that always worked with Sylene—I persuaded her to show me to her room. I spotted the purse the minute I walked through the door. It was sitting right on the lamp table—"

"Go on! Hurry!"

"The secret was in distracting her. I told her that her boss was calling for her. When she went downstairs to answer his supposed summons, I fled down the back fire escape."

"Oh, but you are clever, Evart!" cooed Trudy. "You deserve a trophy. We shall have our ranch, and Ann Marie shall have her Nelson. All things cometh to him who plotteth." She gave a triumphant hoot.

As she talked, Trudy was emptying the handbag item by item. "Here is Mrs. Oakum's money, though it looks as though Sylene helped herself to a good portion of it."

"She bought a dress."

Trudy counted. "There's about thirty dollars left. That's enough to put us in the green until we get the insurance money."

She clawed at the purse's lining. "The papers must have shifted. Here, Evart, cut this cloth with your pocketknife."

No papers hid beneath the fabric.

"I don't understand, Evart. I know those documents were here. Sylene's birth certificate and the insurance settlement papers—those papers are worth thirty thousand dollars, Evart! What could have happened to them?"

"I know nothing about the papers, Trudy. I brought your purse to you. That's what you asked me to do. If you misplaced the forms, it isn't my fault."

"Evart Briggs, are you accusing me of—?"

"I'm accusing you of nothing, Trudy. It rather seems the other way around."

"You have been daft since the day we married!"

"And you've been fractious!"

"I've had reason to be! I have waited eighteen years for that insurance money, and if anything happens now to take it from me, I shall not wish to live a minute longer."

"Ah, now you know how I feel about Nelson Curtis,

Mama," Ann Marie soughed. "If I should lose him, I shall not wish to live."

"I expect that life will go right on for both of you whatever happens," Evart postulated.

"I say the papers couldn't have just walked off, Evart!"

"I say if you two are going to argue all day, I'm going to my room," snapped Ann Marie, who looked on life through a mirror and saw only herself. "I'm sick of it. There are more important things to worry about than some dumb old papers."

"Ann Marie is right, Trudy. We must not quarrel."

Trudy glared at him, then turned to her daughter. "Ann Marie, go write a letter to your sister and explain your position with Nelson. And ask her if she took some papers from my purse."

"In any event, she promised to be home in time for her birthday," finished Evart. "The papers would do you no good until then anyway."

CHAPTER Fifteen

Change

Sylene's thoughts raced about, walled in on every side. She had not a cent. All of her resources vanished with the missing purse.

A potpourri of emotions erupted within her. The loss of her money troubled her, but she found no regrets that the ticket was gone. Now she had no means of returning to Trudy Briggs's world, where she was an intrusion. Whatever Sylvia Arlene Oliver's roots, they were not bedded in the Briggs' soil.

The thread of her life was now twisted into two distinct strands: relief and anxiety. She could not go back to Bruceville without a ticket, yet she didn't have the funds to stay at the inn when her temporary job ended. Decision time had been thrust upon her, and she didn't seem to know the solution to anything anymore.

She was grateful that she had placed the birth certificate, along with its accompanying paperwork, in the Bible Nelson sent her. Evart Briggs had paid the Bible no attention; she could not have chosen a safer place for her document. What use she would have for the certificate she did not know, but having it in her possession made her feel better, less vulnerable.

She knelt to pray, and all at once, she knew what she must do. Her choice came easily, for it was obvious. She must go out and look for work. With a clear mind, a strong body, and a birthday looming, surely she would be hired by someone.

As was his pattern, the old-timer came back for the weekend. "The inn is my second home," he asserted. "If I did not come, my friends would miss me. You see, I haven't much time left on this earth, and I must spend it wisely."

Since his baptism, Mr. Hermann had not missed a worship service. He sat beside Sylene. When she prayed, he prayed. When she clapped her hands, he clapped his hands. When she closed her eyes, he closed his eyes.

"What he does is not imitation, Miss Briggs," one of the visiting ministers told her. "He is learning; you are discipling the old fellow."

At noon, when Mr. Hermann came to sit beside her at the long harvest table, Sylene had some questions for him. "Have you lived in this area for a long while, Mr. Hermann?"

"Yes, I have, milady. I have," he replied. "For a half century. Fort Worth is my wife's native city. The city branded her with its brand. It has remodeled, cut, trimmed, and stamped me to its pattern.

"But hark, milady. You can go a long, long way and stay a long, long time. You can cultivate new and strange tastes and smells—fancy foods and a million city odors.

You can educate yourself to the devious paths of concrete and elevators. You can go away to the sea and the mountains. Yes, you can do all that. But if you are from a small town as I was—born and bred there—you are always from a small town. It's in the blood; it's in the bone." He stopped for breath. "But why do you ask?"

"Did you know any Olivers?"

"Um, let me think. That name does ring a bell. Oliver . . . Oliver. It has been a long spell, but there was a young man named Oliver who met some sort of tragic end in an oil field accident. Seems he was working in the middle of the control house, walking over the rundown lines, drawing samples, and all that. Then something went wrong. The salt settler blew off and split the drum—"

None of this made sense to Sylene, but if it involved a man named Oliver, she must listen carefully. "You don't remember the year, Mr. Hermann?"

"Ah, it must have been back about twenty years ago. Let's see. Was it before or after?—anyhow, Mr. Oliver hadn't a chance against the steam and smoke and flame. No, he hadn't a chance. Nor did the others. Four men died."

"Do you remember Mr. Oliver's first name, sir?"

"I don't recall it. One's mind rusts with age."

"Was it Thomas?"

"Now that you mention it, I believe they did call him Tom. Yes, I believe they did."

"Did he have a family?"

"That I don't know. I don't know. All I heard is that this Mr. Oliver was a prince of a man."

"The oil company, is it still in business?"

"That was the Jessup Company, and if my memory serves me faithfully, they closed out about ten years back and went farther west. But why do you ask?"

"Thomas Oliver was my . . . relative."

"A near relative?"

"Yes, sir."

"Then you must have appreciated the company's fair settlement. I'm told they took good care of the survivors of those men."

"I know nothing about that, sir."

"That was the immediate families, of course. It's a pity you weren't immediate."

"And one more question, Mr. Hermann."

"At your service, milady."

"Do you know where a young lady might find a job?"

"A friend of yours?"

"Myself."

"What kind of job are you wanting?"

Sylene shook her head. "I don't know. Anything that is . . . is honest. I haven't any formal training."

"The textile mill hires girls, but the hours are long. The hours are too long."

"I'm not afraid of hard work or long hours."

"The pay is three dollars and fifty cents a week for a seventy-hour, six-day week. That's a nickel an hour. I once worked there myself."

"And I would need lodging. Might I find something to let nearby?"

"There is a boardinghouse, but—" he paused. "No, I could not abide the thoughts of you living in a boarding-house. It isn't fitting for milady. I know where there is a small house but a stone's throw from the factory. That would do. That would do. I could let it out to you, for I own it, you see."

"What would the cost be?"

"Whatever you could afford."

"Would one dollar a week be enough?"

"That would be plentiful. Plentiful. And if you think you would like to work there, I could recommend you for the job. I know Mr. Cross, the supervisor."

"I would appreciate it."

"It's mighty hard work, milady. Why don't you marry the preacher man and let him take care of you? If I read his eyes right, he'd like that."

"He . . . he is interested in someone else."

"With that glad look in his eye for you? Hardly! Hardly!"

The conversation concerning the job came at an opportune time. The next week, the maid returned to her housekeeping duties at the inn, curtailing Sylene's employment.

CHAPTER Sixteen

Roommate

The letter from Ann Marie came as Sylene collected her small store of personal belongings for the trip to her new lodging. Not taking the time to open it, she placed it in her Bible with the certificate.

Situated at the end of a narrow, unevenly cobbled street, Mr. Hermann's cabin consisted of one room, built from rough cedar and roofed with hand-split shakes. The remnants of unpainted shutters hung on crude leather hinges to shield the windows from the weather. The floor was packed dirt. At one end of the room, a battered tin stovepipe protruded through the wall. A bunk bed was nailed against one corner. Cobwebs swayed under their burden of dust. But Sylene's heart found no complaint. This was a place to lay her head, and she appreciated it.

"Not a palace," the old-timer said, "but you'll have a little breathing space. And it's a far cry better than the boardinghouse. I stocked you up with a few groceries to get started. There's extra oil for the lamp. I'll come by at the end of each week to check up on you and collect the rent money. If you have a need, let me know. Let me know. I think I'll take myself to the public park for a while. You know, there is an aristocracy to the public parks and even of the vagabonds who live there. Yes, the park bench beckons me, milady." He took his shabby steamer trunk and departed.

It was Thursday evening. Sylene's employment at the factory didn't commence until Monday morning. That gave her three days to get settled. She had food. She had shelter. And she had a job. The sudden severance of all life's ties brought her a free, almost joyous feeling. She would "bother" no one. She would have time to read her mail. Time to study the papers from the purse. Time to enjoy Nelson's Bible. Her life was her own.

She dusted the room, straightened the bed, and hung her good dress on a wooden peg. Then she lighted the lamp and sat down to read Ann Marie's letter.

Dear Sylene,

I hope that my letter finds you in health. Chuckie was bitten by a spider, but he is doing well. Mother and Father are happily planning to move to the new ranch in September. I am out of my mind with excitement, for the place will have a parlor large enough to host my upcoming wedding.

Oh, I am so in love, Sylene! With Nelson Curtis. My heart is so full I think it will splash over. This man, this adorable knight of shining flawlessness, has swept out of sight all other men I have ever known. I wouldn't have believed there was anyone like Nelson in the whole world. They say everybody goes through life searching for their other half, and I know that Nelson is my other half. At last, I have found him!

I cannot bear to wait a year for my Nelson! I will not be happy until I am in his arms forever. That will be heaven. I am hoping to talk him into a Christmas wedding, and that shouldn't be hard since he worships me. I will be seventeen by then.

When he is here, I cannot take my eyes from his gorgeous face. I feel I want to go on looking forever. When I think of him, I am plunged into a dreamlike daze. It is so lovely with him sitting at the table—all of us together—with him grinning and nodding and winking at me.

The very last time he came, he brought me a box of sweets. They were delicious! I can't wait until he comes again, for he will get a surprise. Mother bought me some lip paint and nail polish. I can hardly wait to fix up just for him and see his delighted expression!

Of course, when you come home, Nelson will treat you kindly, too, for that is just Nelson. He is a true gentleman. But you mustn't think he means anything personal by it. Nelson is mine, and Mother says you shall not interfere with my happiness. Mother once had a bad experience in love, and she will see that history does not repeat itself.

Well, do let us hear from you, Sylene. Mother thinks you may have the papers that we need— they have something to do with our getting the ranch—and she would like you to bring them to us. If you cannot come, send them special delivery.

Your sister,
Ann Marie

Sylene read the letter again to see if she could have misinterpreted its meaning. But she hadn't. If she needed a final twisting of the knife in her wounded life, this was it.

Time went strangely out of focus for her. She stood on the shore of the present with the past surging toward her. Some of the waves were days and some were years and some were merely minutes. How dismal, how colorless, how meaningless the canvas of her life suddenly had become. *It's like dying*, she thought, *only I still breathe.* She sat fixed, gazing sightlessly at the pages with a pitiful joylessness, imploring something to shelter her from reality.

O heaven, she sighed, *I didn't know that I cared so much! I cannot bear this—I cannot!*

The quiet and soothing peace she had felt two hours ago had departed. She had a roommate now, a weakening, sapping, subversive roommate, as relentless and deadly as a cobra's coils. It would lie beside her at night, awaking with her in the morning. She would drink it with her water and eat it with her bread.

Her old antagonist, the Shadow, had moved in with her.

CHAPTER Seventeen

Annie

Most nights have a definite end and most days have a definite beginning, but Sylene's had neither. They were continuous, the one blending into the other with no line of demarcation except that the darkness eventually paled against the sunlight bleeding through the shutters.

Sylene drudged through time, serving distaff and spindle, these denizens of the textile world, but her musings turned inward, hardly perceiving the scenes around her and caring for them not at all. She worked in the factory but was not of it. The necessary conversations she held with her peers were against her will.

While the threads spun and twined, she stood apathetically beside her machine. The work stretched over the hours. A hasty lunch was eaten as the workers stood without leaving their positions.

The ceaselessness of the work tried Sylene severely. While others stopped to drink ale or exchange a few remarks of gossip, for her there was no respite. The incessant whirring and quivering, in which every fiber of her body participated, threw her into a stupefied reverie. Her arms worked independently of her consciousness. She hardly knew where she was.

Yet Sylene kept going. If she could not fill her part, she would have to leave, and this contingency held terror. Where would she turn if she lost her job? She had no family and no friends save the old-timer. At closing time, her knees trembled so wretchedly with the shaking of the machine that she could scarcely walk.

At week's end, Mr. Hermann came to collect his rent. His clothes had taken on a seedy cast not formerly common to him, and his hair was dirty. He'd neglected his razor. "How did milady manage her first week?" he inquired.

So utterly exhausted was Sylene that she hadn't the strength to speak loudly. "I . . . I made it," she whispered. "It is much harder than the work at the inn."

"Ah, Mr. Arvilla misses you, and so do I. So do I. He wishes he could afford to hire two maids, but alas, his business will not support another employee. But now that I have learned to pray, I will pray for you. Yes, I'll pray for you."

Coming from Mr. Hermann, they were precious words, and Sylene took special joy in them. As a new convert, Mr. Hermann was developing his spiritual muscles. She hoped that she was growing, too.

For a month, the old-timer came each week, bringing bread and milk—and his stories told in his dry, unhurried way. Then one Saturday, he did not show up. It had rained all week, and Sylene blamed the inclement weather for his absence. She hadn't realized that she would miss him so sorely. Without his visit, the day stretched to eternal proportions, vacant, empty. Her very soul ached with the loneliness.

On Tuesday of the following week, Sylene's body reached the limits of its endurance. Lack of rest and nourishment came to collect their dues. She fainted at her machine, and when the world swam back into focus, a woman from the cutting table to her right bent over her solicitously, bathing her face with a damp, threadbare rag.

"Are you all right, dear child?"

"Yes, I . . . I think so. What happened?"

"Perhaps you overheated. Do you feel ill?"

"Only . . . weak."

"Where do you live?"

"Two blocks east."

"I will help you to your home. Will any of your family be there?"

"I—no. I live alone. But . . . I must work. I can't go home." Sylene tried to stand, but her legs threatened to buckle again.

"Best you take off for the rest of the day. Mayhap you will feel stouter tomorrow."

"Oh, I hope so."

The woman, who introduced herself as Annie, half carried and half led Sylene to her tenant's shack. She made her comfortable on the bunk bed and brought a cup of water. Here, unexpected and as yet half comprehended, was aid from a stranger who had no cause at all to give her succor and assistance. Sylene was grateful.

"You have a dandy place here," Annie said.

"It belongs to Mr. Hermann. I am only renting."

"I remember Mr. Hermann. He was a foreman at the

factory when I first started to work there. An unselfish man, he. He would part his lunch with those of us who had none. You are most blessed to have a room of your own, Miss—I don't believe I know your name."

"Arlene. Arlene Oliver."

"That's a bonny name."

"Thank you."

"I live over at the boardinghouse, where there's lice, vice, and mice. Boardinghouses are wretched places unless you happen to like boiled cabbage soup and cheap meat at every meal. I've dreamed many a night of having a house of my own. But, of course, it will ne'er happen. Why, it took me six whole months to save up the money for a pair of silk stockings!"

"You must go back to work now, Mrs. Annie," Sylene urged. "On no account must you lose a wage to see to my comfort. I will be okay. Truly, I will."

"I cannot leave you just yet," Annie said. "You are peaked, and you seem to have a fever. I will fetch you some broth."

Night came, and Sylene was no better. Annie spread a quilt on the floor and slept beside her. By morning, Sylene was too weak to rise.

"Please," whispered Sylene, "return to your job."

"I will put in my time and come back," Annie promised. "Don't try to get up while I'm gone."

"But you must go back to your . . . your own life."

"My own life?" Annie chuckled. "I have no life. What a relief it is to be away from the louse house for a span!"

That evening, Annie brought her pillow and a thin pad for sleeping, and as the days wore on to week's end, Sylene learned more and more about her. She had once been married, she told Sylene; she married a poor man, but they were happy. Their one child, a daughter, was still-born. Then her young husband had been killed in an accident, leaving her to fend for herself. With no resources and no training, she had gone to work at the mill and had been there ever since. "I . . . I suppose I'll be there until I die," she concluded.

"I'll be there with you," Sylene said.

A week later, Sylene was still ailing. She fretted that her strength crept back so slowly. "How will I pay my rent?" she worried.

"If I wouldn't be a bother to you, I could move in with you and help with the rent," offered Annie. "Oh, it is so much more pleasant here than at the common house, where we must abide those sunk in sloth and rotted with loose living. I would be glad to share expenses."

"If it is agreeable with Mr. Hermann, I shall welcome you," Sylene replied. "Our spirits agree, yours and mine. We will ask the owner about it when he comes."

"Oh, that would be heaven!" Annie clapped her hands, a wide smile blooming on her face. "To be away from the cursing and gaming and . . . and the drinking. I had quite given up all hope of ever having a peaceful place to lay my head."

Annie, Sylene determined, had a shadow, too. Had it something to do with the loss of her husband? The dead baby? With Annie here, her own Shadow would have less freedom to molest her. Shadows, she'd learned, didn't like company, crowds, or conversation. Shadows were isolationists.

The blow came on Friday. Sylene's boss sent a letter by Annie. Sylene was terminated from her present employment due to "physical inability to perform the required duties successfully." She would not be, stated the notice, reconsidered or rehired at a future date.

Sylene wept scalding tears. Not only did she not know who she was, she also questioned what she was: a worthless and discarded thing, a bit of flotsam on the tide of fate. She couldn't even hold a job. What would become of her now?

Annie wrapped her arms about Sylene. "Dear, dear child," she crooned. "You are not to fret. Annie is strong of body and mind. Annie has been battered but not beaten. Annie has had but few raisins of good fortune in the tasteless dough of existence, but Annie has survived. Annie will pay the rent. In more than twenty years, I have had no such peace and comfort as I find right here. God does work in mysterious ways, His wonders to perform!"

CHAPTER Eighteen

The Funeral

Sylene was not happy. It wasn't proper for Annie to work to support her; she wasn't Annie's obligation.

She had told Annie nothing of her own background, of the certificate, or of the Shadow. Each time she made up her mind to offer the guarded confidence, something arose within her to block the exposé. Her problems would only add to Annie's burdens, and the poor widow had enough as it was.

Mr. Hermann had not been back to garner his money, but Sylene was certain he would not mind her sharing the quarters with Annie. Mr. Hermann had three dollars stashed away in a bottle on the apple crate shelf, awaiting him now. And when, the following Saturday, the knock came, Sylene was sure that it was Mr. Hermann. He'd come for the rent. She swung the door open, ready to greet him, anxious for news from the inn.

But the man standing before her was not Mr. Hermann. Mr. Arvilla himself stood in the opening, looking somber and distressed. "Miss Briggs," he began, "I regret to inform you that we have lost our friend, Mr. Felix Hermann. The night watchman found his body in the park last evening."

"Oh," Sylene caught the frame of the door for support as waves of shock blanked out thought, "w . . . what happened?"

"No one knows for sure, but Mr. Hermann had been having pains in his chest. He was a veteran of the Civil War and suffered some severe injuries back then. He hid his suffering well, but by and by pain takes its toll on the human body.

"When Mr. Hermann told me that he had let his house out to you, I suspected that he moved under a bridge or to the city park. With the rent money, he stayed a couple of days a week at the inn—often I let him stay three for the price of two—to get food and a bath. He likely ate little the rest of the week.

"As you know, it has rained a good deal lately. Felix may have gotten wet and developed consumption. He had a dreadful cough the last time he came to the inn. Whatever the case, he must have known that he wouldn't be in this world for long. The funeral arrangements he made for himself were in his pocket, along with the money for his burial."

Sylene bit her lower lip, willing the action to squelch her tears. "I can't bear to think that he . . . he suffered on my account. He gave up his home—for me?"

"That would have been his greatest pleasure. Felix really had little to live for. After his conversion to Christianity, he was ready to go to a better world. I believe he really wished to die."

"But . . . I will miss him so!"

"We all will. He wishes the young preacher who sometimes speaks at the inn, Nelson Curtis, to conduct his services, and he asked that 'milady Sylene Briggs' do him the honor of attending his last rites as family. The funeral will be on Monday at the inn as he requested. I'll send a cart for you."

From the doorway, Sylene watched Mr. Arvilla walk away. Then she closed the door and stood motionless, her face buried in her hands. With Mr. Arvilla gone, she could cry now, and crying was all she could do. Why had God heaped upon her so much grief?

"My dear, what troubles you?" asked Annie when she returned from the general store.

"It is Mr. Hermann. He is gone. Dead."

"And we will be obliged to move—"

"Oh, I don't know! I don't know what will happen to me. To us. But Monday, I will go to his funeral. He has asked that I be there."

"I would go with you, Arlene, but I dare not miss work," Annie said. "I received a severe flogging for that one day of absence."

"You must stay and work. I will go."

The prospect was not a pleasant one. Almost Sylene had succeeded in erasing Nelson Curtis's face from her mind, the memory of him from her heart. She hadn't thought of him for days. To fulfill Mr. Hermann's last wish would throw her back into his company. Nelson had merely given her his friendship—a comfortable gift—and she made the mistake of accepting it. According to Ann Marie, she was the chosen one, though Sylene could not imagine Ann Marie as the wife of a minister. However, she'd learned that whatever Ann Marie set her mind to, Ann Marie got, be it butcher, baker, or candlestick maker— or Nelson Curtis. Would Nelson bring Ann Marie, his future bride, to Mr. Hermann's funeral with him?

Sylene ate little, slept little, spoke little on Sunday. "If you are strong enough, we will go to church," Annie suggested. "It might bring comfort."

"I . . . I believe I will stay here today," Sylene declined. "Tomorrow will be a stressful day, and I still feel very weak."

"Then I will not leave you."

Sylene had never attended a funeral; she had no mourning clothes to wear. The blue dress was her one garment of distinction, and she would wear that. Mr. Hermann had liked it; he would want her to wear it for him. As for Nelson Curtis, she would avoid him entirely.

The dray came for her at ten o'clock on Monday morning. She tucked her Bible beneath her arm and left a note for Annie saying that she might spend the night at the inn if Mr. Arvilla insisted. In any case, Annie was not to worry over her.

Nelson Curtis was there when Sylene arrived. His mother had accompanied him. When his eyes found the Bible, they lighted up, torturing Sylene with misgivings. Should she have left the Bible behind? Now that he was committed to Ann Marie, shouldn't she offer to return the Book? He would want to record his marriage and the names of their children therein.

Mrs. Curtis ran immediately to Sylene's side; her arm stole gently around her. "Miss Briggs!" she beamed, "there has not been a day since you left that I have not thought about you and wished for you! Are . . . are you well, dear one?"

"I have been ill," Sylene admitted, "but I am stronger now."

"Ah, I knew it. In my spirit," breathed Mrs. Curtis, "I knew that something was amiss. I have prayed for you incessantly. And so has Nelson."

"I got the letter from Ann Marie."

"Yes, Nelson went down for a visit, and—"

Mr. Arvilla interrupted the conversation. "We are ready to seat you, Miss Briggs," he said. "Since you are all the 'family' Mr. Hermann had, I will be pleased to usher you to the front."

Sylene expected to be seated beside the wife of Felix Hermann and was eager to meet the woman Mr. Hermann spoke of with such fondness. But to her disappointment, Mrs. Hermann was not there.

The memorial service was lovely. Nelson Curtis talked about "The Tabernacle and the Temple." As the children of Israel journeyed through the wilderness to their Promised Land, they were granted a tabernacle. The tent was temporary, portable, and subject to deterioration by age and weather, he explained. By the time they reached Canaan, the skins were frazzled and worn. But once they had crossed Jordan, God let them build a permanent house: a temple, splendorous and lasting. Mr. Hermann, Nelson said, had folded his old tent for the last time. Today, he was rejoicing in God's temple, a permanent dwelling, garnished with gold and precious stones. Nelson then made mention of Mr. Hermann as an "eleventh hour" Christian led to Christ through the godly example of a young lady he had met at the inn, one Sylene Briggs, whom he had loved and respected.

At the end of the service, Mr. Arvilla slipped a letter to

Sylene. "I found this in Felix's room," he said. "It is addressed to you." Sylene tucked it in her Bible.

"But what about Mr. Hermann's wife?" Sylene asked Mr. Arvilla. "Why did she not come?"

"His wife?"

"Yes, he said—"

"Felix had no wife. She died twenty-five years ago. Felix lived alone. Oh, I think he often pretended that she was yet alive; he enjoyed bringing her back and arguing with her in his mind. Felix pretended a lot. He died clutching a picture of her. But he is with her today, and we will bury him beside her."

So Mr. Hermann had a shadow, too. Did everyone have a shadow? Now the Shadow couldn't reach Mr. Hermann.

It was hard not to envy him.

CHAPTER Nineteen

The Birthday

At Mr. Arvilla's insistence, Sylene stayed the night in her old room at the inn. The bed was as smooth as she had made it with her own hands on the morning of leaving. She'd quite forgotten its comforts.

In the incoherent multitude of her emotions, she knelt at the bedside, wet eyed. "Mr. Hermann, if I had known, I would not have taken your house!" The words burst bitterly from her mouth as she broke into gusts of sobbing that shook her thin frame. "Better that I go than you. And if I could have known that your wife was gone—oh! I could have been more patient with you!"

She slept no more than three hours. Her nerves fluttered. The daily army of milk wagons at dawn found her awake. She wished nothing greater than to return to Annie. Simple, sweet Annie. There was safety there, safety for her heart.

By the morning light, she remembered Mr. Hermann's letter and read it. In shaky handwriting and with many misspelled words, he penned: "M'lady, if I am in heaven, it is becuse of you. Therfoure, I wish you to have all my earth's goods wich is not much. Just the little ole house is all. I am gone to a better one. A freind, F. Hermann."

Sylene cried, her tears a broth of grief and thankfulness. Mr. Hermann's benevolence meant no more rent for Annie. Annie could save her money for a new winter coat. Annie would probably cry, too, when she learned she would never have to return to the dread boardinghouse.

At breakfast, to her discomfort, Sylene found that Mrs. Curtis and Nelson had also stayed at the inn. Mrs. Curtis greeted her gently, asking after her night's rest. "I am worried about you, Sylene," she said. "You don't look well this morning."

"I am . . . fine." But during the meal, Sylene found herself growing queasy. Each mouthful of food stuck in her throat, rebelling against digestion. *You will not faint, Sylene,* she commanded herself, but her head grew lighter and dizziness engulfed her. She started from the room but sank into a hornblende chair near the door.

Nelson sprang to his feet, covering the distance between them in three leaps. He grasped her hand in both of his. "Precious girl, you are ill—"

She tried to withdraw her hand. "Please, Ann Marie will be angry—"

"We are not concerned with Ann Marie now. We are concerned for your welfare. You are not in health, Sylene. You have became as thin as a reed and hollow-cheeked since I last saw you. I don't like the dark circles under your eyes. You must let me get you to Uncle Richard. My uncle is a doctor—"

"No, really. I will be fine." She clenched her lips, mortified with herself for her weakness.

Mrs. Curtis had joined her son. "Mother," he said, "persuade Miss Briggs to bow to reason. We must get her to Uncle Richard."

"Doctors . . . cost—"

"Nelson's uncle is a very good physician," Mrs. Curtis prompted. "He will charge us nothing. Now let me tell you what I want to do. I want to take you home with me for a week to take care of you. After that, you may return to your job or go home to your folks, whatever you prefer. At present, you are in no physical condition to do either."

"Please. I'd rather . . . " she wanted to say *die*. But Mrs. Curtis was right. In her condition, she was not able to care for herself. Yet how could she bear the dread weight of hours and hours in Nelson's presence?

Another wave of faintness seized her. "I will go," she finished weakly, "but I have no other dress than this."

"I have a treadle, and I will make some day dresses for you," Mrs. Curtis promised.

"And I need to let Annie know—"

"Annie?"

"The lady who rooms with me. She will worry."

"We will send word to her, dear."

Nelson made arrangements that they should catch the stagecoach for Cleburne an hour after noon. He was solicitous and cheerful, almost as though he were glad that her disability cast her into his care.

The trip was a blur, and Sylene lapsed into listlessness, feeling miles away from her body. Her spirit had returned to Annie. She clutched the Bible as though her life depended on her holding it.

Hours later when her mind cleared, she was tucked in

bed with Mrs. Curtis beside her. "The doctor came," Nelson's mother smiled. "He diagnosed total exhaustion. He says that you need rest and nourishing food. In a few days you will be fit as a fiddle."

"What day is it?" asked Sylene.

"It is Thursday, September 2."

"Oh!" Sylene gasped, "It is my birthday!"

"September 2 is your birthday?" A small pain crossed Mrs. Curtis's brow.

"Yes. I was born in 1880. I am eighteen years old today."

"Happy birthday!" Mrs. Curtis congratulated. "I will bake a cake, and we will celebrate. Nelson will be delighted!"

"Please don't trouble yourself for me."

"It will be no trouble at all. This is a special day for me, too. It is . . . it would have been my wedding anniversary. I think I have some candles. I hope that you will be strong enough to sit in the parlor with us—and perhaps take a short walk with Nelson in the garden."

"I probably shouldn't try to walk . . . yet."

The struggle raged fearfully; her own heart was so strongly drawn to Mrs. Curtis's son against her conscience that she tried to fortify her resolution by every means in her power. She had come to the Curtis household with a made-up mind. On no account would she do anything that might cause suspicion for Ann Marie.

But that evening, when she sat beside Nelson and he spread a towel upon her lap for the eating of her birthday cake, she was inwardly swollen with a renewal of sentiments that she had not quite reckoned with. Their corpses, which had laid inanimate in the crevices of her soul, awoke and came together as in a resurrection. She felt herself drifting into acquiescence, as helpless as a weak swimmer in a strong undertow. Every seesaw of her breath, every wave of her blood, every pulse singing in her ears revolted against her scrupulousness. She found herself wanting to snatch the pleasures of his nearness before the iron teeth of time could shut upon her. That was love's counsel, and in almost a horror of ecstasy, Sylene confusedly sensed that, despite her hours of self-chastisement, wrestling, and schemes to spurn Nelson's attentiveness, love's counsel would prevail.

It is wrong! I am sinning against my own sister! Yet I cannot help myself. Oh, my heart! Oh, a voice within her cried, *God, help me!*

CHAPTER Twenty

The Fleeing of
the Shadow

Doctor Richard Curtis told the Curtises that an "infection" deeper than physical had brought Sylene to her present condition. A sore of the spirit, so to speak, whose origin could be traced to some unconfessed secret gnawed at the peace of the girl's mind. He had met with it on other occasions. No surgery could mend it, no medicines cure it, but if the agitation were not removed, the girl would continue to waste away. Mrs. Curtis had commandeered Nelson to join her in prayer, relying upon the promise "if two of you shall agree on earth as touching any thing that they shall ask, it shall be done."

After the birthday celebration, Nelson left the room but not before he had brushed Sylene's hand with his lips. The quiver of her body was visible, and something like a sob solidified in her throat.

Mrs. Curtis pulled a chair near Sylene. "Dear child, I love you," she said tenderly, "and I want to see you well and happy. My brother-in-law, the doctor, tells me that your mind is bothered with troubles bigger than your young shoulders can carry. Won't you let me help you with them?"

The Shadow leered at Sylene. *You would not dare to betray me*, it seemed to taunt. *This is our secret.* And had Sylene been stronger of body and will, she would never have shared her burdens. But with a woman as understanding as Mrs. Curtis, Sylene deemed that she had nothing to prove and nothing to lose by unloading herself. If she did not unburden her heart, she would fall beneath her cargo.

"It is hard . . ."

"Go ahead. We will take it to the Master."

"For as long as I can remember, there has been this . . . this Shadow about my life," Sylene commenced. "I think I first noticed it when I was about six years old. My mother—or the woman who posed as my mother—told me I was a 'bother' to her." As Sylene talked, she gained confidence. The Shadow didn't choke her or strike her or take her breath away; indeed, it seemed to grovel. "I noticed that my mother favored my sisters, who were ages four and two at the time.

"At school I worked hard to make my mother proud of me, but nothing I did was good enough. My sisters earned the praise, the compliments.

"I pretended that it didn't matter, and I stayed from underfoot as much as possible. Often I was punished for the misdeeds of the others because their explanations were accepted and believed above mine. Eventually, I ceased trying to defend myself. In my childish mind, I was somehow flawed, defective." She went on, as if to forestall any words of sympathy.

"This Shadow, it was like another being, a self I didn't know, had never known, and couldn't know. At times I thought it was a . . . a wall of darkness bent on keeping me from finding my true identity. I . . . I know I am not making sense, Mrs. Curtis, but bear with me."

"You are making sense, dear. And the emptying of your soul is good for you. We want you to be whole again."

"At the age of fifteen, I began working for an elderly neighbor—I think I told you this before—and I was away from home for two years. My mother—or supposed mother—was happier when I was away."

"And what of your father, dear? I don't believe you have mentioned him."

"He was a good man, but when he dared to take my side, my mother became enraged. I have reason to believe that he is not my father at all. But who is my father? And where is he?"

"We shall pray about that, too."

"The future is guarded by the Shadow even as the gate of Eden was guarded when Adam and Eve were expelled. I cannot marry, for the man I wed might think me one person when I am really another.

"I am ashamed, and I cannot tell you why. I don't know why. I am someone else. I don't know who I am. I never knew. Oh, shall I never know, shall I never understand why I am not myself? I don't know where I belong. It is an awful feeling not to know that you belong somewhere or to someone." There, she'd admitted it! "I am sure that I am living under a name that is not my own!"

"The enemy of our souls likes to torment us," broached Mrs. Curtis. "Your mother may have been betrayed or misused, and you were caught in the backlash—"

"But I must know," cried Sylene, "and she will not tell me. When we came to the city four months ago, she forgot her purse and left it at the station. I was in possession of it, and . . . and I found something—" Sylene's voice broke, her lips trembled.

"What did you find, dear?"

"In the lining of the purse was my birth certificate. She had hidden it there."

"Why would she hide it?"

"The man's name on the certificate is not the name of the man who reared me. My name isn't even Briggs!"

"What did you do with the certificate?"

"I put it in the . . . in Nelson's Bible."

Nelson had come into the room. "I came to see how the princess is feeling," he sallied, his tone gentle.

"Nelson, please get Sylene's Bible from her room for us," his mother requested. "We are trying to get some matters straightened out for her. I feel . . . that God will help us."

Nelson went for the Bible and handed it to Sylene. In the back of Sylene's mind, the Shadow danced and hissed. *No! No!* She had second thoughts. Had she done the wrong thing by divulging this information to a stranger? No, Mrs. Curtis wasn't a stranger; she was a friend.

But the friend will soon be Ann Marie's mother-in-law, Sylene! You are cutting your own throat! She hadn't considered this fact until now. The thought brought a new panic, a suffocating fear.

"Oh, I . . . I can't. I can't tell—" she gasped, the remnant of a break in her voice. "If my mother finds out—!"

"Your mother should have been honest with you years ago, Sylene. You are eighteen now and no longer a child.

She can cause you no harm legally."

Nelson had not left the room. "And if she does try," he said, "I have another uncle who is a lawyer!"

Sylene's eyes met his. "But I don't want to cause problems between you and Ann Marie."

Nelson's face wore a confused frown. "You won't cause problems between Ann Marie and myself. Why should you?"

Slowly Sylene removed the folded document from the Bible. Uncertainty still plagued her. This might constitute a betrayal of her mother. It might heap more wrath upon her head. "According to this birth certificate, my father's name was . . . was Oliver."

"Oliver what, dear?"

"That was his surname."

Mrs. Curtis's body jerked forward in the chair. "Oliver?"

"Thomas Josiah Oliver."

"No!" Mrs. Curtis's hands flew to her face, covering it. "It—it can't be."

"That's what it says here."

"I was married to Thomas Josiah Oliver on September 2, 1879."

"My mother's maiden name was Jones," Sylene said.

"Yes. And her given name?" The question caught on snags of excitement.

"Trudy Bessanne."

"I . . . I—" Mrs. Curtis reeled. "Nelson, please bring me some cold water."

"Are you all right, Mother?" Nelson rushed to her side. "You are as pale as a ghost!"

"No. I mean, yes. I can't believe it, even though I have

135

prayed for all these years . . ."

"On the certificate, my name is—" Sylene started to read the name.

"I know your name!" Bess Curtis cried. "You are Sylvia Arlene."

"But how do you know, Mother?" Nelson asked.

Bess laughed and cried, then laughed again.

"You do? You . . . you know who I am?" Now Sylene was crying, too. Or was she laughing?

"I know! Oh, yes, I know! You belong to me. I am your mother! Trudy is my sister. My Tom was killed before you were born. Trudy came to stay with me until my baby's birth. When you were born, Trudy ran away with you, taking the papers with her. I have searched for her—for you—all these years and never found either. Oh, how I have grieved! And now . . . and now! . . ."

The tears of mother and daughter mingled, tears of joy, healing tears. "Oh, my precious baby!" wept Bess Curtis. "I've found you!"

"My mother!" wept Sylene, now in Bess's arms. "I know who I am!"

The entire evening passed like a dream, a timeless moment of beauty. For all her life, Sylene would treasure the memory of this day, the day she miraculously found herself.

And the Shadow fled.

CHAPTER **Twenty-One**

A Joyous Day

The feeling of wholeness was still with Sylene when she awakened the next morning. She sucked in a deep breath of air, sweet with the scent of fall, and her mouth curved into a smile. *Mother . . . I have a real mother . . .*

There were a few clouds moving about the sky, covering and uncovering the sun. But that did not matter. No cloud could blot out Sylene's precious possession, that of knowing who she was. Today nothing could quell her deep satisfaction, her fullness of heart.

"Good morning, Miss Oliver," Nelson greeted at breakfast. "How does it feel to be eighteen and have a new identity?"

"Wonderful!" she beamed. "I wrote 'Oliver' a hundred times this morning so I would remember my own name!"

"May I see the papers you had last evening, Arlene?" Bess Curtis asked. "I was so excited about finding you that I forgot about the page that should be attached to the birth certificate. It is an important directive concerning you."

Sylene went for the papers and handed them to her mother.

"Yes! Thank God they are intact!" Bess cheered. "We will file the claim for you at once."

"The claim?"

"Your father left you well set, Arlene. The settlement will amount to some thirty thousand dollars. Invested well, it should take care of you for life. As your mother, I am included in the compensation, but I shall not take a penny. I have a comfortable living and haven't a need for it. Today, you are a wealthy woman."

Thirty thousand dollars. Mrs. Oakum's forty dollars had seemed a great fortune, but thirty thousand? Sylene could not comprehend such riches. If she worked at double her wage—to make ten cents an hour—for the rest of her life, she could not earn that amount. What would she do with so much money?

She supposed that she would never marry. She'd let her heart "out of school" once—to the man Ann Marie would wed—and she would guard it carefully from now on. She might be a nurse. Or a seamstress. Or manage an orphanage for homeless children.

She had Mr. Hermann's little hut, too. That, she decided, she would give to Annie. Annie would have a home of her own. And what a thrill it would be to bring happiness to another!

"Should I . . . should I . . . write and tell Trudy Briggs?"

"No. There is no need. She will come here looking for you soon enough. I shall tell her myself."

"Thank you."

"I wish you could have known your father, Arlene. He was a prince, a Christian of the highest order. He would be proud of his daughter. You favor him. Even in spirit, you are so much like him."

"I should like to have known him."

"I'll get in the attic and find pictures."

Nelson broke in. "Well, Arlene, my darling, we will take a walk in the garden after breakfast." He reached across the table and placed his hand on hers. "The red runners are in bloom. Red roses for—"

"No, I . . ." Askance, Sylene withdrew her hand abruptly, "I . . . can't—"

"Then we will have a visit inside. We have a lot to discuss, you and I."

He's going to tell me about his wedding, reasoned Sylene. *And I don't want to hear about it. Oh, I do want him and Ann Marie to be happy, but I don't want to think about it today. Please, God, let me enjoy this one day of gladness.*

How exposed she would be to temptation in Nelson's presence! She was in danger of envying her sister, coveting the man Ann Marie had won through her cunning and her deceit. Jealousy might even pounce upon her. *Walking in the garden with Nelson would fling me into the chief crisis of my life,* she decided.

"Go on, you two! Have your fellowship," grinned Bess Curtis. "I will clean the kitchen. The plates will never have a happier scrubbing. I've put up with a lovelorn Solomon for four months now. That's long enough." She shooed them from the room.

Nelson settled Sylene on the settee, then situated himself very close. A ray of light shone through a small opening in the curtain and formed a golden staff which stretched across Sylene's skirt. "Are you comfortable, dear?"

"Y . . . yes, but I—" She must tell him that she had no right to his company, his attention. Ann Marie would be very upset if she knew that they were sitting together.

"Let me tell you my side of the story, Sylene—uh, Arlene. Then if you have objections, you can voice them."

I would never tell him that his marrying Ann Marie will be a mistake . . .

"About three months ago, I discovered that I was in love with a beautiful girl."

That's when he met Ann Marie . . .

"I didn't dare admit it to myself at first, but it has run away with me now, absolutely and forever. I can't look at life, I can't turn any way, I can't think of anything in which I don't see my precious one."

Ann Marie . . .

"I went to God about the matter, for God must give His approval to all that I do."

Ann Marie, an answer to prayer?

"The more I saw of my beloved, the more dearly I loved her. I lent my soul to much searching. What I am, I mused, she will be. What I cannot be, she cannot be. I must never neglect her or hurt her or even forget to consider her first. God forbid such a crime!"

But sitting here with me, you must not be thinking of your espoused now. This would hurt her . . .

"God sent you into my life, dear Arlene."

So that you might meet my younger sister . . .

He moved nearer, and for one moment brought his lips to her cheek. "He sent you to me so that I might have a future filled with . . . with a little heaven on earth. Do you understand? I am in love."

"Yes." She spoke in the dull voice of a dull heart, slow

and labored. "I . . . I hope that you will be happy."

A curtain had fallen between them. Tears surged to her eyes though she tried to staunch them.

"Are you . . . not happy?" His hand was on hers.

"I . . . I cannot stay . . . in this room . . . with you . . . just now." She hurried outside. She needed air. And space. And relief from his closeness. The ordeal had strained every nerve in her body.

Nelson was soon close at her heels, for she walked slowly and without purpose. She turned at hearing his footsteps, but the recognition of his presence made no difference to her. She only half felt the touch of his hand, very light upon her shoulder, a touch given but once and swiftly withdrawn. Her face burned.

"Wait, Arlene. I'm sorry! I supposed that you felt the same way that I feel. Your eyes . . . I thought I saw devotion in them. I supposed that you . . . that you loved me, too—"

"Oh, I did! I do! That's the problem!"

"The problem? I cannot see a problem, darling. Will you not be my wife?"

"I cannot." Only her pupils betrayed the pathos of her inward suffering.

"But why?"

"It is one of the commandments! 'Thou shalt not steal.' I cannot take you from Ann Marie. It would be a . . . sin."

"From Ann Marie?"

"She wrote about your plans to marry her."

"She *what*?"

"I have the letter. In the Bible."

"Oh, my darling! You think—you thought—that I was in love with *Ann Marie*?"

141

"Yes . . . that is, she said that you were. That you brought candy . . . and . . . and—"

"The candy was for you! I asked her to see that you got it when you returned home." He shook his head. "Ann Marie thought I was calling on *her*? I thought I made it clear—oh my darling, how you must have suffered!"

Sylene swayed, and Nelson caught her, enclosing her waist with his arm to support her.

The sudden vision of Nelson's passion for herself so moved her that, beginning with one slow tear and then following with another, her face streamed with rivers of joy, of thankfulness, for the happiness that lay ahead. How could so many good things happen in so brief a span?

At last it came, that faint, first catch of breath which surprises a child whose weeping has been checked and whose hurt comforted. Nelson clasped her hand, entwining his fingers with hers. "Which are my fingers and which are yours?" he joked. "They are very much mixed."

"They are all yours," said she. "Now and forever."

He picked a red rose and placed it in her hair.

Was she breathing air—or rapture?

CHAPTER Twenty-Two

Travel Plans

"I used the money in the purse to get ready for Ann Marie's wedding," Trudy Briggs informed her husband.

"Trudy! You spent thirty dollars for—?"

"Well, we bought some other things, too, Evart. But they were necessary for Ann Marie's self-esteem and happiness. So I sold Spotsie's calf to get the funds for the trip Ann Marie and I plan to make to Cleburne this week. Ann Marie wants to see her fiancé, Nelson Curtis, and I am going to find Sylene."

"You have dallied around for four months and haven't produced the papers we need. I won't return without them. Sylene's birthday passed a month ago. We should be in fine fettle by now, and we're only growing poorer."

"It doesn't help, Trudy, that you wasted thirty dollars and now you're selling off our livestock," reprimanded Evart.

"What is thirty dollars and a scrawny calf against thirty thousand dollars, Evart Briggs? Huh? Tell me that!"

she retorted. "You've never been smart when it came to financial matters. Listen, if I don't find Sylene, she just might claim all that money for herself—"

"She can't claim your part of the money, Trudy. If the papers list her mother as a beneficiary—and you are her mother—it would be illegal for her to take it. I am intelligent enough to know that. You have naught to worry about."

This conversation was another of the pills Trudy had been obliged to swallow. Self-analysis, that rude guest who drops in, as unbidden and unwelcome as a constable, to set all one's favorite vanities out of doors and evict one's self-complacency, had intruded upon her conscience. "If you must know, Evart, I have plenty to worry about. Sylene is not my child by birth. And what if . . . what if she finds her real mother?"

Evart's mouth fell open. "What drivel are you talking, Trudy? Have you taken leave of your senses? Of course, Sylene is your child."

"I am telling the truth, Evart," she said, waving her hand in the impatience of a person whose tortures cause every instant to feel an hour. "I am not Sylene's legal mother. I was not married to Thomas Oliver. He was my sister's husband. Sylene was born to my sister."

"But you told me—"

"I lied to you. I took Sylene from my sister when she was newborn. Her name is Sylvia Arlene Oliver. But since I have reared her, her mother's portion shall come to me. Unless . . . unless Sylene has discovered the truth on the certificate and—"

"Oh, Trudy! Trudy! Don't you know you could go to prison for life for kidnapping a child? It is a crime! Why weren't you honest with me? It might have prevented years of misunderstanding and woe for both myself and Sylene."

"Don't you see, Evart? I couldn't risk losing the money."

"Some things are much more important than money. Virtue. Truth. A noble character."

"Eighteen years of my life as caretaker beg a proper collection," insisted Trudy stubbornly. "I shall have my pot of gold."

The gold, however, interested Ann Marie but little. She had built sand castles around Nelson Curtis, and she was ready to occupy them. Into her traveling bag went her eye paints, lip dyes, and face powders. "We'll be in the new house in time for my wedding, won't we, Mama?"

"To be sure, Ann Marie. Don't fret your pretty head."

"And, Mama, when we get to Cleburne, we must take a room at the big Liberty Hotel. I asked Nelson about a nice place to stay, and that's where he recommended. He probably has in mind honeymooning there. I want to get a look at the place.

"And here's what I want you to do: early in the evening, feign yourself tired and hie yourself to the hotel. I'll stay behind at the Curtis' house and dawdle around until after dark. Then Nelson will be obliged to escort me to the hotel by moonlight. Ooh! Can you think of anything more romantic? The almanac shows a full moon for this week. I plan to get Nelson to set a definite date for our marriage while we are there. Wouldn't a Christmas wedding be just perfect? If Sylene is home by then, she can be my maid of honor." Ann Marie rambled on, fluttering her tapered hands, their scarlet tips flying about as she gestured. "Oh, I do hope that Nelson gives me a bouquet of roses.

Flowers bring a good feeling, a proudish feeling. Roses mean true love."

"Calm down, Ann Marie," exhorted Trudy. "You will wear yourself out before we even get there."

"But, Mama, you don't understand! Nobody knows, nobody understands what it means to be in love with Nelson Curtis. It's . . . it's—" her voice failed completely.

Trudy sighed, a heavy sigh. "And nobody understands what it means for an older sister to marry the man you have your heart set upon. That's what happened to me."

When Evart walked away, or what part of the conversation he'd heard, no longer concerned Trudy Briggs.

"But it won't happen to me!" Ann Marie declared with steady-eyed effrontery, speaking more to herself than to her mother.

CHAPTER Twenty-Three

Beyond the Shadow

Along the street, the trees were turning. Banners of crimson, yellow, and burgundy flaunted where the foliage had been sunburned and heat corroded. Autumn had come with her clarifying elixirs and her fever-cooling evenings.

As the sun moved westward, Bess Curtis carried her chair to the porch and sat in the shade of the morning glory vine. She had never been happier. Her prayers had been answered; she had found her daughter.

Sweet warmth centered in the upper region of her body and softly filtered through her being. Today, the delicious future held no doubts or shadows for her. For eighteen years, she hadn't missed a single day petitioning her heavenly Father for the return of her child. Now, she'd had her miracle. The dark moments of the past fled before a radiance that suffused her heart like the flaming javelins of an equatorial sunrise.

They that sow in tears shall reap in joy. She had

read that scripture many times, but now she lived it. She was drinking—yes, gulping—from the cup of joy.

A carriage stopped in the narrow street before her house, and a girl alighted, swinging her sunhat by the ribbon. Her linen gown dipped frighteningly low in the front; her lips were as red as fresh blood. She hurried toward the porch.

Bess stood, walking to meet her. "May I help you?"

"Is this the Curtis residence?" The question came in a rush as the hurried turning of a book's pages to get at the plot quickly.

"It is," Bess smiled.

The girl turned and beckoned to someone in the coach. "This is the right place, Mama," she summoned.

A woman stepped out, giving the driver a coin. As she neared the house, Bess recognized her. This was her sister, Trudy, the woman who had stolen her baby.

"You are Mrs. Curtis, Nelson's mother?" Ann Marie asked.

"Yes."

"I am your son Nelson's fiancée," she announced. "I am sure that he has mentioned me to you. Perhaps he has even told you of our wedding plans. We have been corresponding for some time now, though I haven't heard from him in some days. I fear someone is tampering with my mail.

"My name is Ann Marie, and this is my mother, Trudy Briggs. We are on a trip to visit my sister. Our coach stopped here, so I implored Mama to allow me to make a call on my future mother-in-law. I knew you'd wish to meet me." Bess couldn't tell whether the girl's red sear of a lip curved or curled. "If we may come in for a few minutes?"

"Certainly." Bess stepped aside, inviting them to take

a chair in the sitting room. "May I get you a glass of lemonade?"

"Yes, thanks," Ann Marie said, speaking for both of them.

Bess's mind spun. The moment of truth had come. Apparently, her sister did not recognize her. That gave Bess an advantage.

"Is Nelson not here?" Ann Marie asked, facing about.

How will I tell her? Bess considered. *And how will she react?*

"No," she said. "He is away on a trip."

"Oh, he told me about his travels. How exciting! I look forward to traveling with him." Unable to keep her hands still, she tapped her painted nails on the arm of the chair, making a clicking noise. "When will he return from his trip?"

"I'm not just sure—"

"We shall plan to stay in town until Nelson returns, won't we, Mama?"

"Perhaps we can come back by," offered Trudy. "And maybe you can help us, Mrs. Curtis. I am looking for my daughter, Sylene Briggs. Nelson informed us that she had spent the night at your house at one time. Have you any idea where she might be living at the present time?"

"I have," Bess replied, her self-restraint tested.

"Could you please give me her address? We've lost track of her, it seems."

"I shall give you the information you are seeking, Mrs. Briggs, if you will answer one question for me. What is the purpose of your visit with Sylene?"

"We have some financial matters that need attention. She is my daughter and . . . and—"

"Yes?"

"She has some legal papers that I must have. They were in my purse, and I have reason to believe that she took them."

"And this is why you seek her?"

"That is the primary reason, yes."

"If I should tell you that I have those papers here, would you still feel an urgency to find her?"

"Not an urgency, no. The papers are dated material, you see, and I thought I would have them in time—"

"Yes, I see. I know all about the documents."

"You . . . do?" Trudy's usually colorful cheeks turned as pale as ivory.

"I'm glad you have come, Trudy," Bess said levelly, "for I have somewhat to say to you. I am your sister, Bessanne, though my late husband called me Bess. I am the sister you wronged eighteen years ago."

Surprise, disbelief, and dismay chased each other across Trudy's features. For once she flinched under the full blow of that news. They sat silent, the longest of moments.

"You thought that I took Tom from you. The truth is, Tom never loved you. It was I that he adored from the start. Had I not married him, he would not have chosen you.

"When my baby was born, you took advantage of my illness and my grief. Why? Because you knew that there was a great deal of money involved. The love of money is the root of all evil, so says the Good Book. So you took my daughter, my one little ewe lamb, and fled."

Trudy half started up, then involuntarily sank back into her seat.

"You might have told her some of these things. You might have let her know who her real mother was and who her false mother was. You might have given her a chance to know herself. But you didn't tell her anything which did not serve your own purposes.

"You covered your trail fairly well, but a criminal will leave behind some mark of his crime, either by accident or by intent. You left marks all along life's path with your neglect of my daughter, your partiality to your own children. Had Arlene not found the certificate, she would eventually have figured you out.

"You played a hard game for Arlene's money, and you came near to winning. For a time you deluded my poor child, killing her sunny nature with your toxin. It was by chance that we found each other, Arlene and I. No, it wasn't by chance. It was by the ordination of God. The mercies of the Almighty on the innocent saved my child from ruination at your hands."

Ann Marie tapped her toe on the floor, making known her boredom, showing her unconcern for the skeletons in the family closet. "Mama, why don't you go back to the hotel," she said. "I'll stay and visit awhile."

Bess ignored the interruption. "After you kidnapped my baby, Trudy, I did as many other women have done: I got on the best I could. Tom made provisions for my welfare, and I was comfortable. But I never gave up the hope of finding Arlene. I believed that the truth would come out some day.

"After a few lonely years, God put a kind and understanding man in my life, Nelson's noble father. His prayers joined mine for Arlene's safe return. I only wish he could have lived to know that I found my daughter.

Perhaps the angels will tell him."

Bess paused, still smiling. "I want to thank you, Trudy, for the gracious lady that Arlene has become. You see, if I had reared her, I would likely have spoiled her to a ferment! Adversity made a queen of her. Hardness made her gentle, affliction gave her inner strength. You had her for eighteen years, but I shall have her for the rest of my life. I shall grow old and feeble basking in the love of a caring daughter. Like Arlene says, we have much catching up to do!

"But the best of all good fortune was when Nelson, my wonderful stepson, chose my own daughter as his wife—"

Ann Marie jumped from her chair with a gasping exclamation on her stricken face. "Nelson . . . married Sylene?" Her black-lined eyes sank.

"Yes, she was the apple of his eye from the first time he saw her. He never loved anyone else," Bess said.

"But, Mama, you told me—!" screamed Ann Marie with a wild mingle of frustrated wrath and outraged dignity. Out of her blanched face, her eyes stared wide and piteous.

"And now I have a double blessing, you see. My daughter is also my daughter-in-law. Nelson and Arlene have gone away for a lovely honeymoon."

"Let's go, Mama," Ann Marie whined, now pathetically. "There's nothing to gain by staying longer."

Trudy sat for a time weeping, her eyes downcast, her fingers braiding and unbraiding. "Oh, how will we ever manage? The lease on the old house is due, and we've no money to pay. We will be put out—"

"I'm coming to that part, Trudy," Bess said. "When my beautiful daughter collected her insurance money, she set aside five thousand dollars for you. She hoped that you might buy a new home with it."

"But I . . . I don't deserve it."

"That is true. You don't deserve it, Trudy. But my child has a heart of gold, and I hope that my heart may be as pure. We talked about the past, Arlene and I. Your terrible sin against us brought a dark shadow to each of our lives, stalking us and sabotaging our happiness. We lived with those shadows for eighteen years. Then we found each other. And we have forgiven you.

"Now we are beyond the Shadow forever."

About the Author

This is author LAJOYCE MARTIN'S thirty-first fiction book. She has written wholesome Christian literature for over thirty-five years, yet her love for good words has not diminished. She is a busy pastor's wife, speaker, and spoiler of grandchildren. However, she always makes time to write one more chapter . . . and to find one more friend.

OTHER BOOKS *by LaJoyce Martin*

The Harris Family Saga:
To Love a Bent-Winged Angel
Love's Mended Wings
Love's Golden Wings
When Love Filled the Gap
To Love a Runaway
A Single Worry
Two Scars Against One
The Fiddler's Song
The Artist's Quest
To Say Goodbye

Pioneer Romance:
Another Vow
Brother Harry and the Hobo
Destiny's Winding Road
Heart-Shaped Pieces
Light in the Evening Time
Love's Velvet Chains
Mister B's Land
The Postmark
The Wooden Heart
To Strike a Match
The Watchdog
A Promise to Papa

Historical Romance:
So Swift the Storm
So Long the Night

Historical Novel:
Thread's End
The Watchdog

Western:
The Other Side of Jordan
To Even the Score

Path of Promise:
The Broken Bow
Ordered Steps

Children's Short Stories:
Batteries for My Flashlight
Cookies that Don't Crumble
Oh, If Only the Animals in the Bible Could Talk!

Nonfiction:
Alpha-Toons
And They All Lived Happily Ever After
Coriander Seed and Honey
Heroes, Sheroes, and a Few Zeroes
I'm Coming Apart, Lord!
Little Words Make a Big Difference
Mother Eve's Garden Club

Order from:

Pentecostal Publishing House
8855 Dunn Road
Hazelwood, MO 63042-2299